A Killer Opening

An Amelia Ferver Mystery

Matilda Adler

First published by Matilda Adler in 2022

Copyright © Matilda Adler 2022

All rights reserved. No part of this publication may be reproduced, stored or transmitted in any form or by any means, electronic, mechanical, photocopying, recording, scanning, or otherwise without written permission from the publisher. It is illegal to copy this book, post it to a website, or distribute it by any other means without permission.

This novel is entirely a work of fiction. The names, characters and incidents portrayed in it are the work of the author's imagination. Any resemblance to actual persons, living or dead, events or localities is entirely coincidental.

Matilda Adler asserts the moral right to be identified as the author of this work.

No portion of this book may be reproduced in any form without written permission from the publisher or author, except as permitted by U.S. copyright law.

Paperback ISBN: 9798785109940

For my mother, Paddie, who gave me my first myste
novel, then sat beside me on the sofa watching Mi
Marple and Hercule Poirot until we both got squa
eyes.

PROLOGUE

It was the first Thursday of June 1994, three hundred and sixty-three days after the day that changed Amelia's life.

On the day that changed everything, Alfred Boustred, the family's ancient, snow-capped solicitor, accompanied Amelia, her mother Maud, and Oliver Kent in their limousine to a funeral service, then on to a well-attended wake.

Alfred had left the wake promptly to prepare for the Will reading, leaving Amelia, Maud, and Oliver to round up the stragglers, then silently trudge the half mile from Berkley Square to the offices of Boustred & Co in Grosvenor Square.

On arrival, a sour-faced reed of a secretary ushered them into Alfred's office, where Amelia had taken her place on one of three unforgiving mahogany visitor chairs that stood facing a tatty, old, leather-topped desk, behind which Alfred had begun reading his late client's Last Will and Testament. He read it aloud, with surprising vigour and impressive linguistic acrobatics.

This was no ordinary Will.

This was the Will of Sebastian Ferdinand Dunnicliffe Ferver, Amelia's Uncle Seb; a man who had been her rock and the last familial connection to her father, Maynard Ferver.

No more than ten minutes into the reading, shifting on the frightful mahogany chair and trying fruitlessly to find a comfortable position, Amelia learned that she had inherited an island, a townhouse in Berkeley Square, and a yacht named *As You Like It* moored somewhere on the French Riviera. Oliver, who was sitting to her left, burst into gales of spite-filled laughter, while Maud, who was seated to her right, seethed, speechless with rage.

The townhouse was lovely, all Chinese rugs and Louis XIV furniture, and located in Amelia's favourite part of town. The yacht... well, you might say that in her almost thirty years on this blue planet, Amelia had yet to locate her sea legs. But the island...

Her heart flipped like a kid on a trampoline while her scalp tingled at the very thought of El Pedrusco.

Uncle Seb's island, you see, was *not* one of the hundreds of tiny and cold Hebridean islands their ancestors migrated south from in a desperate bid to escape the impossibly long winters, with days so short that if you blinked you might miss them. The way Uncle Seb had described those islands to a ten-year-old Amelia had her imagining life inside an old black, woollen sock.

No, Sebastian's island—a mere three kilometres long by two kilometres wide at its broadest point and admittedly insignificant when compared to its more famous neighbours—was perfect. A perfect, stunningly beautiful, and reassuringly uninhabited—except for a handful of eccentric artists, two dozen goats, and the occasional flamingo—jewel in the heart of the Mediterranean Sea.

However, two minutes after this welcome revelation in the Boustred & Co offices, came an equal and opposite one. There were to be three conditions to the bequest, and on hearing what they were, her scalp tingle became a shiver of trepidation.

'Impossible!' Maud cried. 'A dangerous, foolhardy task, set by a delinquent with no thought for the consequences!'

Amelia ignored her mother's histrionics. Maud would see danger in a bowl of soup. Instead, Amelia sat, hands laid flat against her cheeks, wondering.

If she were to accept the challenge it would be the greatest risk she had taken in her life. At her mother's knee she had learned to run from the merest whiff of risk. She had never once gambled, not even on the Grand National: a race on which even the most puritanical of the nation had a little flutter. But not Amelia, for if she was renowned for anything, it was caution; a painful, obsessive zest for caution.

Her eyes stung with tears. She had been tossed a much-needed lifeline, a reprieve from a miserable month in which her carefully constructed world had crumbled around her. And now, with uncharacteristic cruelty, that lifeline had been snatched away, as if her uncle, the one man she had trusted above all others, had sneaked up behind her and whipped the blue-grey, hand-woven, Chinese rug in his Berkeley Square townhouse out from under her feet.

She knew why he had done it. Hadn't he been nagging her to 'live a little,' almost as often as her mother had beseeched her to choose safety over adventure? Amelia had known then, just as she knew now, that he was right to remind her that behind every door was not a serial killer, and more to the point, on every street corner was not a kidnapper. 'Loosen your grip on life!' he had told her. 'Lest you throttle the best years out of it.'

Tears balanced on her lashes, not quite daring to spill over. Never in a million years would she have believed her wonderful rock of an uncle would force her hand in this way. *But perhaps,* she thought, *when he wrote that Will, he was unaware of my current torment.*

Her chest felt tight, like the breath was being squeezed out of her lungs. Quickly, she scanned the room for something solid, something that would calm her beleaguered nerves. Books! The walls of the office were lined with shelves, and she began mentally picking out and counting off all the tomes with green spines. *One...two...ah, there's another...* Eventually Amelia's heart slowed, and she returned to the present.

'When was it written?' she'd whispered through sandpaper when Alfred eventually finished speaking. Though barely audible, her words exploded bomb-like into the silent office. Maud's face convulsed, then slackened. Oliver froze, stiff with guilt.

'I attended him at home, at his bedside, two weeks ago. He had recently returned to London to put his affairs in order,' Mr Boustred replied, unbothered, or perhaps unaware of the tension building across his desk's scarred surface. 'It seems he knew death was imminent.'

Oliver shifted, preparing to explain, but it was all too much for Amelia. She scraped back her chair, rose to her feet, anger pouring off her even as her tears still hovered on her lashes. But beneath the anger she could feel an iceberg approaching, bringing with it a chilling sense of betrayal. 'Oliver, you were here for two weeks and didn't contact me?' she asked. 'Tell me you didn't know what hell I was going through. At least give me that!' she begged. 'I wrote on the third of May and thought that perhaps—with his fanatical aversion to the telephone, and the island's sporadic postal service—my letter never reached him ...for why else wouldn't he come?'

'He did come, you wretched child. He came home for *you!*' Oliver snapped, his face pinched in indignation. 'He came home to this cold, grimy, cacophony of negativity just to make sure you would get the life you needed. Not the safe little nothing of a life you've chosen! It is a priceless gift,' he continued, his voice vibrating.

'What good is this gift? I have a year, Oliver. A year in which I will either try and fail to best his ridiculous, pointless challenge; a challenge that even the great Sebastian Ferver did not manage to achieve in his whole life. Or I will *not* try. Either way, when the year is done, I will have nothing...not even him!' Amelia's voice broke on the last word.

Oliver's body jerked, as if from a blow. Not that she cared.

She had wiped his usual sneer of superiority right off his face, and she was glad. His face flushed red beneath its bronzed surface.

Amelia started to move toward the door. She'd had enough of this day, enough of this office and enough of Oliver Kent, so instead of waiting for whatever tirade he was about to disgorge, she turned to the doorway to leave.

Amelia's father, Maynard Ferver, had disappeared in the deepest, darkest part of Africa when she was eight years old. A hysterical Maud had fallen into a vat of scotch to drown her sorrows, only deigning to leave her bed for the gala openings of her plays. Everything else—food, work, entertainment...*everything*—took place in her suite of rooms on the fourth floor of their once stunning, now dilapidated, old Georgian townhouse in Mayfair.

The drip, drip of years of neurotic negativity from a permanently drunk Maud had convinced her young daughter of two truths. First, that one should never take any risks, never go exploring, never truly live, lest something irreversible happen; and second, that Maud's happiness, what little she allowed herself, was reliant on Amelia's ongoing servitude.

From the age of eight, Amelia had been nursemaid, cook, housekeeper, receptionist, and a whole lot more to Maud's Mrs Rochester. On her darkest days, Amelia considered meting out Mrs Rochester's fate on her mother, but most of the time she dutifully dedicated herself to her role of caretaker.

She was miserable. Only school holidays on Uncle Seb's private island, with her two best friends Daisy and Leo, had ever managed to soothe her ruptured soul.

And then came the debacle of Daisy's kidnapping. Afterwards, Maud had deteriorated further, convincing herself that either she or Amelia would be next. Amelia had been sixteen by then, and so it was natural that she should add typist, personal assistant, wardrobe mistress and, eventually, ghost-writer to her Maud-focused repertoire. All to keep a roof over their heads and to babysit an increasingly unstable Maud.

And all the while she was sabotaging me behind my back, Amelia reminded herself, as if she could ever forget.

She crossed the office. Amelia had no idea where she was headed, not then. But by the time she reached home some hours later, a home she had shared with Maud ever since she was a baby, she knew.

Amelia Ferver was going to grasp this challenge with both hands, because she knew if she did not, her life would be exactly what Oliver had accused her of.

A life unlived.

And even Amelia, with her head firmly buried in the sand for so long, knew that that was absolutely the worst kind of life anyone could have.

CHAPTER ONE

On that Thursday, eleven months and twenty-eight days later, Amelia woke beneath white cotton sheets with the Mediterranean sun pouring in through the powder-blue shuttered windows of her very own newly constructed boutique hotel.

Soon after she woke, her dogs, Chesterfield—aka Chessie—and Tulip, rose from their beds on the floor, stretched luxuriantly, then clambered up onto Amelia's bed to join her. Next to arrive was Oliver who, apparently sensing her D-Day jitters from way down the hall, had deposited her favourite breakfast out on her balcony's wrought iron table, thankfully without uttering a word. As she ate it, Amelia stared blankly over the clifftops and the aquamarine sea to the west, and then on to her very own almost-mountain, La Colina Alta, to the north.

After downing two cups of tea and devouring three slices of marmalade laden toast, she descended the staircase, sliding her hand down the smooth surface of the olive wood banister sitting atop a stained-glass balustrade, as she moved down from the galleried landing and into the grand entrance hall below.

This morning, Amelia did not notice how the light reflected the blues, greens, and aquamarines of the coloured glass up into the cathedral ceiling, nor did she notice how the vein that ran like waves through the expansive marble floor exactly matched the shade of the polished olive-wood stair rail.

She did not notice any of the beauty of her hotel or the island beyond its walls because she had a problem. A problem that the next few days would either kill or cure.

Eleven months and twenty-eight days breaks down to eight-thousand seven-hundred and twelve hours, or five hundred and twenty-one thousand, one-hundred seconds.

Amelia loved numbers; they were predictable. Words were predictable too, of course, solid, sometimes even poetic, but they could be ambiguous, and today of all days, Amelia needed certainty over beauty, safety over the poetic. Which was why, in her anxiety, Amelia was doing what she always did when she was nervous. She was counting.

Taking a deep breath that did nothing to abate the ever-present twisting sensation in her chest, Amelia—'Lia' to only her closest of friends—headed to the sanctuary of her office.

'Is Daisy's room ready? Have all the changes she requested been made?' Amelia asked Oliver. He was a middle-aged man with sun-bronzed skin, and in this moment, he was draped like a sunbathing lizard across one of the comfortable visitor chairs in front of her desk.

Oliver and Amelia had been working all morning, and now, with the yacht carrying the first of her guests due at any moment, they were going over the final details for the two-hundred and seventy-third time.

Only the keenest of observers would have caught the slight tremor in Amelia's voice. Throughout the morning, trepidation had warred with excitement on this day which was sure to be high on drama, not least from her now estranged mother, Maud. *But the ship, the guests, are a necessary evil if I am to win the prize.*

Today was the culmination of twelve months-' worth of blood, sweat, and tears, and it looked like she and her Man Friday might pull off the miracle they had prayed for.

All the same, Amelia couldn't shake the heart pounding sense of foreboding which had dumped a boulder in the pit of her stomach. It was a boulder she hadn't felt since the morning she had walked out of Alfred Boustred's office, instinctively accepting her uncle's challenge to build a healing hotel on El Pedrusco, his jewel of an island in the Mediterranean.

Amelia took a moment to study the man sprawled in the chair in front of her. He was still handsome for his age, which simple mathematics told her was not the fifty something he looked. His raven-dark hair, aquiline nose and perpetual sneer was somehow reminiscent of those grainy black and white photographs she had seen of 'Lucky' Lucan, the English Earl who had murdered the nanny and battered his wife with an iron pipe before disappearing in a puff of smoke.

Today, Oliver was dressed in the brand-new hotel uniform of crisp white shorts and a daffodil-yellow polo shirt. His whiskey eyes were warm, though they seldom stayed that way for long. Oliver was a military man, just like her uncle, though he had been an officer in the Coldstream Guards, while Sebastian Ferver had been career navy.

The two men had met at the Victory Services Club, a stone's throw from Hyde Park, and had been firm friends and companions from that first meeting until the day of her uncle's death. Amelia had always assumed they had been more than friends, but she would never ask and risk embarrassing a man she had known for most of her life—a man who had, with workmanlike efficiency, swabbed her childhood cuts and grazed knees.

Oliver had been at Sebastian Ferver's side for more than twenty years. Almost a year earlier, he had walked solemn and dignified beside his friend's coffin as it wended its way through Highgate Cemetery to the Ferver family plot. He had been the only person left standing in the pouring rain at Amelia's side—Maud and Alfred had sheltered in the limousine—long after the other mourners had been ferried back to his townhouse for what Oliver had called 'tea and wake.'

That day and Uncle Seb's blasted stipulations! Amelia thought, pulling one of the orchids from the vase on her desk and fiddling with its speckled white petals.

Everything depended on her old schoolfriend, now Hollywood's darling, being present at the grand opening. Oliver knew that, though at that moment, slouched low in his chair, he did not appear to be taking the upcoming opening quite as seriously as she.

'Everything has been arranged in accordance with Daisy's agent's *detailed* instructions,' Oliver answered in his haughtiest tone, which wasn't as haughty as he thought. Not if you had lived a lifetime as Maud Lavender's daughter.

'Are you sure?' Amelia asked again, her voice brittle with desperation. If this opening didn't go according to plan, she would lose everything they had both worked so hard to build.

Not just lose it, but according to Uncle Seb's dratted Will, it would be carved up into tiny pieces to be auctioned off to the highest bidder and the proceeds distributed to a host of worthy environmental charities hell bent on saving the world. Amelia had nothing against the world per se, but she couldn't bear to think what that would mean for her beloved El Pedrusco.

'I have allocated her the Palm Suite,' Oliver relented. 'It is the largest room we have, with triple aspect views of the sea, the mountain, the artists' community and the lighthouse beyond. The bed has been shifted so that she can easily reach the light switch. A torch, candles, and a book of matches have been placed on the nightstand, and Ms. Forrester's desperate need for Fort Knox security, on an island with more goats than people, has been assuaged by the installation of three separate locks on the suite's entrance door as well as on each of the windows, not least the miniature bathroom window that even a toddler couldn't squeeze itself through.

'I am sure our preparations will be more than satisfactory to meet the demands of Hollywood's favourite princess.' Oliver could not have sounded more like Uncle Seb at that moment, and Amelia's chest tightened in grief. He was being facetious; no one with ears could have missed that fact. He wasn't supposed to use it with her, however. They had a deal. But she would allow it, just this once, because it was her two-hundred and seventy-third time asking that question.

'And Maud's room?' she dared to ask, the weight of her mother's imminent arrival for the pre-opening VIP preview heavy in her gut, because Maud Lavender was not only famous for the exquisitely crafted plots of her West End and Broadway productions, but also for her alcohol drenched, sometimes sharp-wittedly hilarious, always devastatingly acid, commentary on life. Maud hated everything almost as much as she feared everything, and she did not hold back in expressing that hatred.

Amelia would gladly have foregone the dubious pleasure of her mother's presence at the gala if the blasted woman hadn't been her only access to Herb Hogan: the most influential —and definitely the sleaziest—member of the entertainment industry press pack. She knew Maud wouldn't think of inviting him without receiving her very own engraved invitation.

'I have checked Ms. Lavender's room myself. She will have no *genuine* complaints on her arrival.' They both knew her mother would find plenty to complain about in the Dorchester, so there was little hope of Amelia's little island hotel passing muster.

For Amelia, Uncle Seb's bequest, and subsequent rug-pulling challenge, couldn't have come at a better—or worse, depending on your perspective—time. Of course, she would have preferred the dear old fool to have stayed alive, so he could comfort her when her mother had been revealed to be more of a monster than even Amelia could have believed.

'The musical chairs have been accomplished. Stop worrying!' Oliver growled. 'Pau is safe in his lighthouse and David has moved to Sawubona and Tantriana's bungalow so the pair can be on hand to provide spiritual guidance to your guests at any time, day or night.' Was it Amelia's imagination, or was Oliver taking a swipe at their strange guru and his muse? Uncle Sebastian had picked them up on his travels—who knew where or why?—but their combined skills, a fusion of African and South-Asian, were a godsend to the newly installed proprietor of a healing hotel.

'Price Whitney will have the blue suite next to Daisy, and Leo will have the yellow suite on her other side. Wendy will have the second room in your mother's suite, so she can be at your mother's beck and call twenty-four hours a day, and the slimeball, Herb Hogan, has requested a bungalow.'

'He wouldn't prefer a suite in the main building?' Amelia asked, surprised. The bungalows were lovely with their own little gardens and terraces, but they weren't particularly close to the amenities.

'No, apparently the king of the paparazzi is not a people person,' Oliver said, his tone dry, though his lips were twitching. Then magically, Amelia felt a wave of laughter bubble up from deep in her chest, a laugh so silly and instinctive that the boulder in her stomach crumbled.

The moment of humour passed, as it always did with grumpy old Oliver, and Amelia's jitters roared back with a vengeance. The stakes were high. The slightest hitch and she would lose the one stable thing she had left in the world: El Pedrusco.

'Everything will be okay, you know,' Oliver said, his angular face gentling.

'It really does have to be, you know. For both our sakes,' Amelia grumbled, shaking her head, her chocolate bob flowing like water as she did.

According to the solicitor Alfred, the terms of Uncle Seb's Will were legally airtight.

It had all been right there in black and white. In order to inherit everything, bar the life interests in the cottages he had left to each member of the island's artists' community, and a bequest to Oliver that he would only receive on the same conditions as her own, Amelia must in the space of one short year, fulfil her uncle's lifelong dream.

By the first anniversary of the Will reading, she must have built a thirty-room healing hotel on the island, and she must mark the occasion with an opening gala befitting the perfection that was El Pedrusco. And lastly, both of her long lost, but once dearest childhood friends, Daisy Forrester and Leopold Alcott, must be present at the gala opening.

On the day of the funeral, two warring sets of words echoing in her mind, Amelia had made a deal with the Universe. She would do something she had not done since she had climbed the bent old olive tree halfway up the path to the summit of La Colina Alta; she would take a risk in honour of her uncle. If she succeeded, she would be a very wealthy and happy, if utterly exhausted, woman. If she did not, she would surrender to her mother's way of thinking, slink back to London, and return to the safe, unfulfilling world of Maud Lavender.

That was Amelia's motivation for going over their plans for the two-hundred and seventy-third time. As for Oliver, his incentive in this grand project of theirs was that her success would be his success. Oh, he certainly wanted to honour his friend's final wishes, but Sebastian Ferver had dangled a financial carrot in front of him too.

If Amelia succeeded, there was a million pounds sitting in a bank with his name written on it. Their shared goal had provided the single-minded purpose they had needed to drive them further than Amelia had thought possible.

'Ahem.' Oliver's tetchy throat clearing interrupted Amelia's thoughts. 'If you're planning on besting darling Seb's inexplicably complicated and tiresome challenge, you better head for the—' He was interrupted by the sound of approaching footsteps.

Oliver did not utter another word, just scowled and glared at Amelia. He was like a dominant dog, angry and snarling in the face of an approaching intruder. The type of dog you must never be off guard around and must never back down from, or he'll pounce, and you'll end up getting your throat ripped out.

Which was why Amelia's gaze was steady, quietly assertive, as it met his and held. And all the while, the footsteps continued their determined, ominous approach.

CHAPTER TWO

Hackles raised, Amelia and Oliver were enjoying their faux-angry staring competition when David wandered in unannounced and without bothering to knock.

He was dressed in a pair of navy sailing shorts, a cherry-red, pencil-striped shirt, and soft-soled sailing shoes. As always, dapperly dressed with his wavey blond-streaked hair smoothed back with gel, he looked more like a model or actor off the front cover of a yachting magazine than the penniless sailor he claimed to be.

While working on Maud's theatre productions on both sides of the Atlantic, Amelia had met—and had crushes on—enough actors to know how differently they carried themselves when wearing their costumes to when they were in mufti; and David was *never* in mufti.

Amelia was the kind to notice details, so she couldn't help noticing David's little foibles. Every stride he took was long, smooth, and measured, but every few steps his sole would skim along the floor, as if he couldn't resist skating close to the edge. He walked with his hands shoved deep into his pockets, hinting, to Amelia at least, that he had something to hide.

She hadn't quite decided about David. Sure, he looked yummy enough to slather on a chocolate cake, but beneath the frosted icing surface, there was something of the mushy peas about the man.

If Oliver was her Man Friday, that would make David—who had been marooned on her island exactly a month before the coming weekend's grand opening—Robinson Crusoe himself. Though, luckily for him, unlike his fictional forebearer, it seemed that with a little loving care and some chivvying along, his yacht would be salvageable.

'You two have been holed up in this pokey little cave of yours for so long, you seem to have lost track of time,' David drawled, tapping his watch and tutting.

Amelia looked down at her own slim wrist and gasped at what she saw. It was 2 pm, and her guests were due to dock at... 2 pm.

'Are we done duelling?' she asked Oliver, jumping up from her chair, ready to dash to her car. Oliver nodded solemnly, stood up, smoothed his hands down his clothes to remove any creases, then strode out of the room without a word of goodbye, no doubt heading for his Land Cruiser. He had not even acknowledged David, who stood slouched by her office door, smirking. *Mushy peas,* Amelia thought, before saying, 'Okay, I'm off. Will you be here when we get back?'

'Here or on the *Titanic*,' he drawled.

When Oliver had learned that catastrophe had struck David's yacht on its maiden voyage just weeks into his planned 'round-the-world cruise, with customary acidity he rechristened it the *Titanic*.

'Don't bother to hold dinner for me if I'm still off tinkering,' he said, leaning back against the door frame, crossing his legs at his ankles, and shoving his hands still deeper into his pockets. He was lucky Amelia was in a hurry, otherwise she might have reminded him who was working for whom.

The two of them had struck a deal: she needed all hands-on-deck to get ready for the grand opening and he—practically penniless, having spent all his cash on a Friday-afternoon-er of a yacht—had agreed to help in exchange for cash to buy parts.

Amelia wasn't certain how much work David had actually done in the run up to the gala, though while breakfasting on her balcony earlier that morning, she had definitely spotted him with her lighthouse keeper and general factotum, Pau, working together to fix her uncle's ancient tractor.

Tamping down her temper, Amelia grabbed her car keys, scurried past David, and sprinted across the forecourt to her car.

The car tyres spun as Amelia tore down the hotel driveway leaving David Ash bathed in a red haze of Mediterranean laterite dust. She waggled her arm in the air in a belated goodbye just as she cleared the massive olivewood gates, swung the car sharply to the left, then thundered off down the island's only paved road in a hurry to reach the tiny jetty. She was anxious to greet her guests.

The road, which Amelia had nicknamed Highway One back in her teens, spanned almost the full three-kilometre length of the island, and had once been perfectly paved. Extremes in weather, coupled with a general lack of maintenance, had degraded the black-top into the decrepit mess it now was as she slalomed around potholes, palm fronds, and other detritus on her headlong sprint from the main hotel building to the island's unassuming little harbour. She made a mental note to ask David if he and Pau could use the tractor to clear up the road before the party on Saturday.

As Amelia drove, the wind poured over the windscreen, whipping the strands of her normally impeccably dark-chocolate bob in frantic circles around her face like flames dancing in a hearth.

Gone were the greasy locks and extra pounds she'd piled on while she catered to every one of

Maud's whims. A year in the Mediterranean had turned her from anxiety-riddled and overweight to a happy, increasingly confident, curvy, young Liz Taylor lookalike.

Except for today. Today, the anxiety had returned as her uncle's deadline neared. Leo and Daisy needed to be on that boat. And once they were here, Amelia needed them to stay at least until the gala on Saturday. Two days...not much to ask of old friends. Although things had ended rather abruptly with Leo, and she hadn't even set eyes on Daisy in almost fifteen years...

Her hopes of mending both of those relationships over the weekend did sound rather ambitious when she thought about it that way.

One miracle at a time, Amelia...

But magically, as she drove, her body relaxed, and her pounding heart unclenched. She'd never been able to resist this car with its drop top roof, bench seat, and white wall tires. Nor had she ever been able to resist a drive down Highway One, even as a teenager with Daisy and Leo.

As she roared past kilometre two, Amelia thought of how Uncle Sebastian couldn't have provided her with a better distraction if he'd lived to do so himself. It might even have saved her sanity.

You see, Amelia had discovered, a little more than twelve months earlier, that everything she had built her life on was a lie.

As Maud lay like a beached whale, sprawled across her bed one Monday afternoon, Amelia overheard one side of a telephone conversation.

'Oh, Amelia is such a lazy girl. Positively useless I tell you! Her personal hygiene is appalling—never bathes. And she's ballooned to the size of a heifer. If I wasn't here to take care of her, she'd be dead in a week.'

Of course, they'd had a blazing row after Maud had hung up, and during that row Amelia discovered that Maud had been badmouthing and undermining her for years, not even showing an ounce of gratitude for the three plays Amelia had ghost-written when Maud had claimed to be too weak—too traumatised—to write them herself.

'And I did young Leopold Alcott a tremendous favour when I put a stop to your silly little love affair!' Maud had screeched at the height of their exchange. Everything that was said after that was a blur, as if Amelia's mind had seized like an oil-less engine.

Drop it! That's in the past. You have enough on your plate today without bringing up old hurts, Amelia told herself as she rounded the final bend in the road over the brow of a shallow hill. The harbour came into view.

Amelia pulled up at a viewpoint that overlooked the harbour, taking a few moments to ready herself for the onslaught. She opened the car door and walked to the cliff edge. There, moored at the old wooden jetty, right beside David's yacht, stood an old-fashioned dual-masted sailing ship. It had been a romantic treat, in honour of the occasion, for her special guests to arrive at their island hideaway in a Turkish gulet.

For a moment, she stared out across the aqua water at the grey-green cliffs of Mallorca to the north. Over the last few weeks, every time she gazed across the water at the largest of El Pedrusco's siblings, Amelia had felt a sense of doom, like her breath was being choked out of her. *And now the reason for it is here,* she thought, glancing down into the harbour where a group of people were milling around, while the sailors and Oliver offloaded their luggage.

Amelia's guests had arrived. She had done everything in her power to meet her uncle's stipulations. The rest was out of her hands.

By the time Amelia had jumped back into her car and wended her way down the zig-zag road to the harbour, the gaggle of people had surrounded Oliver's Land Cruiser.

There was Daisy, her childhood friend, in all her willowy six-foot, honey-haired, loveliness. She was clothed in her signature, form-fitting evening gown—this one was lilac—Dior sunglasses, and skyscraper sandals that wouldn't last a minute on a hike to the summit of La Colina Alta. Amelia hadn't seen her childhood friend since Daisy had been kidnapped off a London street when they were both sixteen. She had tried to make contact on countless occasions after Daisy was freed, but she had never replied to Amelia's flurry of letters, cards, and phone calls.

It had broken Amelia's teenage heart to think of her friend damaged and alone, but then when Daisy had made it in Hollywood, every photograph and movie had showed a thriving, vibrant young woman, loving every moment of her new life with her father on the other side of the Atlantic. After that, Amelia had decided to save her sympathy for herself.

And there was, of course, Leo, who was standing beside Daisy. They were the final piece to the Sebastian Ferver puzzle, and it was no surprise to Amelia that their presence brought on a dual wave of relief and apprehension.

Relief because both Daisy and Leo setting foot on El Pedrusco and staying until the Saturday gala would fulfil the final stipulation to her uncle's Will, and apprehension because she couldn't imagine what Leo thought of her after Maud's interference. She struggled to meet his gaze.

He was only a smidge taller—six-foot-two—with a slim build, and he wore his cream linen suit like it had been made for him. His caramel hair, with its floppy fringe that seemed to have a life of its own, was mostly hidden by a Panama hat, and though she wasn't close enough to see the startling blue eyes she had fallen in love with as a girl, she imagined them twinkling with unexpressed laughter. When they were flirting teens, that laugh had frogs jumping around in her chest and her knees turning to jelly.

But, as she had learned in that row to end all rows, Maud had taken great pains to put a stop to their burgeoning love affair. He hadn't wanted to come to the opening; she could tell by the tone of his first letter. It had taken every weapon in her considerable arsenal to persuade him. What finally clinched it was her insistence that it had been her uncle's dying wish that he be there.

Leo had a soft heart. He was kind, loyal, and had a quiet strength that suited his name. She hoped Uncle Seb, up there in the heavens, would forgive her little white lie about dying wishes.

Standing a little apart were Sawubona and Tantriana. They'd accompanied the staff to Mallorca and had served as a welcoming committee to her guests as they boarded their floating transportation. They'd stood in for Amelia so she and Oliver could remain on the island to iron out the final details for the upcoming gala.

As usual, Sawubona wore his trademark orange robe with red cord tied around his waist and strange little string sandals on his feet. His hair was jet black and reached almost to the cord at his waist. Amelia thought he looked like Robert Powell when he had played Christ in *Jesus of Nazareth,* though Sawubona's skin was darker, betraying his mixed South-Asian and African ancestry.

And there was Tantriana, his spiritual muse. She was tiny, no more than five feet tall, of South-Asian heritage with dark-copper hennaed hair. She was dressed in a white robe with an orange cord that set off her gleaming almond skin, and she wore a chain of daisies looped crownlike around her head.

And there was the journalist, Herb, wearing what looked like a safari suit, with a pair of binoculars and a telephoto-lensed camera hung around his neck. Beside him was a large man with thinning grey hair, and a body that was padded far more than was healthy. He waved a fat cigar around, complaining about the 'goddamned sun.' Amelia thought he looked like a Texas oil baron on vacation, and she knew immediately it was none other than Price, Daisy's agent, the man who had provided the endless list of requirements on Ms Forrester's behalf.

Oliver was loading cases into the back of his Land Cruiser when a flapping motion caught Amelia's attention. Turning her head, she spotted the person she had been dreading seeing most. Her mother Maud was busy piling bags, files, a giant floppy hat, and what looked like three shoe boxes into the arms of her harried secretary, Wendy Gale.

After she had discovered her mother's duplicity, even before her uncle's death, Amelia had begun to plan her escape. Breaking free of her mother's control had taken a great deal of planning and Wendy had been the ace up Amelia's sleeve.

Wendy was the perfect applicant for the position of Maud Lavender's assistant. She had top notch references from directors and producers of both stage and screen. Amelia had taken to her immediately, though the other woman, who had skin so pale it was like alabaster and hair so white she looked like a Tolkien elf, was timid as a church mouse on first meeting, and hardly improved on further acquaintance. Still, on paper she had been perfect, but Amelia knew her mother would bully poor Wendy so harshly she worried she wouldn't survive. Which was why Amelia had acted against her own best interests and suggested Wendy keep looking for alternative work.

Wendy had resisted, showing more backbone than Amelia had given her credit for. She insisted she would take the job if it was offered to her. When Amelia left the lawyers office the day of Sebastian's funeral, her first call had been to Wendy to organise a final interview with Maud. She was gone before the interview took place, but, as she had predicted, Maud offered Wendy the job. Like all sharks, Maud could spot blood in the water and couldn't resist following its scent.

'Hola!' Amelia called out to her guests as she jumped out of her car and strode across the small harbour to greet them.

Leo's and Daisy's faces were guarded as she approached. They had been three musketeers back in their teens, swallows and amazons running wild on this island, but time and life had built barriers where once there had been none. Not that the tension penetrated Maud's obliviousness as she immediately began to imperiously allocate people to vehicles.

Maud, Daisy and Leo would join Amelia, of course. Price would not be separated from his client so he too would be travelling in the Cadillac. *Lucky it has bench seats.*

The staff, as Maud called them—Wendy, Sawubona and Tantriana, as well as Herb the journalist—would travel with Oliver and the luggage.

As Maud gave directions that were rightfully Amelia's, she heard Herb mutter, 'Go ahead, treat me like a peasant now, but you'll suffer the consequences later. Remember, what goes around, comes around!'

The pile of luggage from the yacht did not seem to be dwindling much as Oliver marched backward and forward, from dock to Land Cruiser, packing them in like he was figuring out a jigsaw puzzle.

'Let's be off,' Maud ordered, not looking at Amelia. She climbed into the front passenger seat and slammed the door shut, leaving the larger-than-life Price Whitney to squish himself into the back with Daisy and Leo. As he settled himself, he reached over the seat behind and patted Amelia clumsily on the shoulder.

'Name's Price Whitney,' he said. 'Named by my old Pa, who always told me that everyone has their price. Said he'd made damn sure I'd never be able forget that one little nugget of wisdom.' Amelia had never before met anyone who felt the need to explain their name.

She knew her own name Amelia was the English version of the German one, Amalia, which meant hardworking and industrious, the exact opposite of what Maud had accused her of being on that phone call thirteen months earlier. She considered recounting the history of her own name but, glancing at Maud's stony face, she thought better of it. No doubt Maud would manage to turn that line of conversation to Amelia's terrible and heartless abandonment of her after the Will reading.

'Don't spare the horses!' Price bellowed from the backseat as Amelia fired up the engine. 'And damned fine horses you have beneath your bonnet, little lady.'

Amelia didn't miss the double meaning in the man's words. She ignored it, but she did not *miss* it. She also decided, in that moment, to do everything she could to avoid EveryoneHasTheirPrice Whitney.

'Do you remember, in our teens, how we used to steal this big, bad beast and go joyriding up and down the island, Daisy?' Amelia asked, smiling into the rear-view mirror at her old chum.

There was no response.

'Daisy?' Amelia called again, a little louder this time.

'Oh...yes...You're quite right,' Daisy murmured in response before turning her face to look out the window, gazing with unseeing eyes at the crew who were readying the ship for departure.

Sighing, Amelia shifted the car into drive and pulled away from the jetty, heading up the twisty road to the clifftop.

The vacant look on Daisy's face reminded her a little of how Maud had looked after the kidnapping. When the teenage Daisy had been taken, Maud—who was also Daisy's godmother—had gone so deep into shock that the doctor had prescribed a sedative to help her sleep. Daisy looked like Maud *after* taking the sedative.

'Did you enjoy the gulet? Was the crossing a smooth one?' she asked, again into the mirror as she swung the big ship of a car out onto Highway One, heading for the hotel. This time she did not rush. They had plenty of time before they began the afternoon's itinerary, and she wanted to take the opportunity to point out some of the island's features as they went.

'Smooth enough,' Leo answered, his voice rough with emotion. They were the first words he had spoken to her since the day, seven years earlier, when he had failed to turn up at their planned date—a date at which Amelia had been certain he would propose to her. Something inside her cracked open at his words. *Smooth enough.* She hoped her explanation of Maud's duplicity would be smooth sailing too. Surely the fact he was here said something.

It was enough for now and, like a warm hug, it gave her the motivation she needed to begin their guided tour. 'Let me explain the layout of the island

and the plan for these next few days before the hoards arrive.

'The yacht is now readying to set sail and it won't be back until Saturday afternoon, when it will deliver the guests to the gala. Until then, we will be like shipwrecked sailors. No telephones, no television, just rest, relaxation, and whatever pampering you fancy,' she told them with a grin.

Maud harumphed, while Daisy continued staring out the window, this time gazing unseeing at La Colina Alta, the almost-mountain. Amelia knew flamingos were wading in the shallows of the lake that lay beneath it.

'The skipper told us we'd be stranded, only the sneaky lowlife did that *after* we'd boarded,' Price said. 'I'm a busy man, lady. So I'm gonna need access to a telephone.'

'Oh no!' Amelia said. 'We promised you a restful, uninterrupted stay, and that's what we will give you, whether you like it or not. The next three days have been meticulously planned as an opportunity for you to see the island's unique attractions, a place where you can get back to nature, free from the distractions and the emotional drain of the real world. We have Sawubona—a world renowned yogi—to offer spiritual guidance, healing treatments, and yoga for your uptight, over-adrenalized bodies. There will be gentle hikes to get your blood pumping, as well as a snorkelling safari around the subterranean caverns; and in the evening, we'll be playing old-fashioned board games and relearning the lost art of conversation after a homegrown vegan dinner.'

'What the hell are you talking about? Who cares about some yogi who, by the way, is *not* world renowned, otherwise I'd be representing him? I've got genuine celebrities up the wazoo who need their hands held, their egos massaged, and more than both of those, they need constant access *to me!*' He turned to Daisy beside him. 'And let's not forget, Daisy, my princess, that I have a telephone meeting with a studio exec on Friday. A very important call!'

Amelia was busy kicking herself for exaggerating Sawubona's credentials when Leo spoke.

'Looks like you're going to be a no show, old chap,' he murmured sardonically, just as the old Leo would have. A whisper of a smile crossed his lips and Amelia felt a flicker of hope in her chest.

'Harrumph...fine, I can be flexible. If I don't get my own phone, I'll just share your office for a few days,' Price said, nodding to himself and looking as if he'd just solved world hunger. 'Just like that, back in the race!'

'No office telephone,' Amelia said, giving a little shrug of apology. 'No electronics at all, I'm afraid.' After only five minutes in his company, Amelia's head was beginning to pound.

'It was all in the brochure, Peppy,' Daisy said, having apparently gifted the ghastly monster of a man with a pet name. 'You did read the brochure, didn't you, darling?'

'Of course, I didn't read the goddamned brochure,' he snapped. 'You said you needed a little getaway, and I made that happen like I always make everything happen. *I* didn't need a little getaway, but *you* said you needed an escort for moral support, so I made that happen too by abandoning my other clients and flying halfway across the world to hold your hand. What in all that would make you think I'd have read the brochure?' Price's voice was rising, and his already ruddy face was turning puce from hypertension. If Amelia hadn't taken an instant dislike to the man, she'd have been worried for his health.

'I didn't read the brochure either, Amelia my love,' Leo galloped gallantly to her rescue. 'So maybe we could pass the time with you telling us about the island?'

With a relieved sigh and a grateful glance—he had no need of a tour guide, of course, having visited this island almost as often as she had over the years—Amelia did just that.

'This road, the island's only road, runs from one end of the island in the east to the other in the west. Right in the centre of the island, a little to the north, over there–' She took her right hand off the steering wheel and waved at the large hill to their right. '–is La Colina Alta, the highest peak on the island. Spreading out behind her, like a mother goose with her gaggle of day-old chicks, is a lumpy blanket of foothills that contour the island and shelter its southern shores from the tramontana wind that pummels the north in the winter months.'

Looking around the car, from Maud's stiff countenance to Daisy's flaccid one, then on to Price's stony one, Amelia realised that the only non-hostile in the vehicle was Leo, so she focused what was left of her guided tour on him.

'The island is the three-kilometre-long and two-kilometre-wide tip of a long-submerged peninsular that once jutted out from the European mainland into the Mediterranean Sea,' she explained. Amelia never tired of the island's apparent contradictions; rugged north with hardy pine trees bent double by the tramontana and heather-covered rocky outcrops, contrasting with the lush palm, cypress, and olive groves of the more temperate south.

'It gets pretty hot in the summer but never goes below freezing in the winter, so I can grow orange and lemon trees, and I have planted a vegetable garden to feed you lot, so I hope you've brought your appetites!'

'Can't wait, love,' Leo said, giving her an encouraging nod, while Maud continued her silent assassination and both Daisy and Price whispered between themselves.

'You will have spotted the lighthouse up on the clifftop. Just to the south of it, nestled in the foothills of La Colina Alta, is a small artists' community,' Amelia continued gamely. 'My general factotum, Pau, lives in the lighthouse. He keeps an eye on it for us, even though it is mostly automated now.' That reminded Amelia of something, and she turned to Leo. 'Do you remember there used to be a fulltime lighthouse keeper, an old fellow with a beard right down to his bellybutton, who would pay us a peseta or two if we helped him out during the holidays?'

'He didn't think we knew he was sneaking off to meet with his smuggler friends down in the caves,' Leo said with a hoot of laughter.

A smiling Amelia did her best to catch Daisy's eyes, but her face was firmly averted.

'Oh, I almost forgot! The flamingos are here. There was a time they were occasional visitors, but now we have an almost full-time resident population.' Again, Amelia waved her hand out of the window in the direction of the mountain with a large saltwater lake spreading out like an A-line skirt at its base. No one was interested; not really. Even Leo's eyes had glazed over, and she was about to give up and surrender to the silence for the last few minutes of their journey, when Price spoke.

'At least you have a beach,' he said, spotting the long white sand of the stunning kilometre-long beach. 'Small mercy I say. We have them bigger and better back home, but at least we can top up our tans while we're stranded here.'

Amelia was relieved when the hotel gate appeared in front of them. 'My uncle, Sebastian Ferver, built his home on the island's sheltered southwest corner, and in recent months, according to his wishes, I've made sweeping changes. I've gutted the original house and turned it into a combined health spa and yoga studio come shrine room for classes, meditation, and silent contemplation. Right next to the health spa I built that red-roofed, white stucco hotel, an art gallery, and a gift shop, both of which showcase the island's arts and crafts. Scattered between the larger buildings, hidden in their own small gardens, are guest bungalows. Inside the circle of buildings, you'll find our central gardens and a pool complex.

'Oliver, Pau, and myself will all be on hand throughout your stay to make certain everything is exactly as it should be,' Amelia said.

'It'd be exactly as it should be if it had a telephone,' Price mumbled, and Daisy laughed. It was a weak, mean, cackling kind of laugh, but it was a laugh nonetheless.

'At the very heart of the hotel's design is the landscaping of the central gardens that links the different buildings together with a network of little outdoor rooms and terraces that provide privacy while still offering interconnectedness.'

When Amelia left the hustle and bustle of London's West End, she hadn't missed it for a moment. Here, on El Pedrusco, her feet were planted firmly on God's earth, and even after losing faith with her mother and *actually* losing her uncle, somehow El Pedrusco had done what it had always managed to do—it had taken her out of her pain and opened her heart. She dearly wished the laterite soil of the hotel gardens would do the same for her guests.

But by the looks on their faces, her words had fallen on deaf ears, like hailstones bouncing off a windscreen. She could imagine Price's heart had plummeted. Maud was silent for the same reason she had been silent throughout the car ride: she was sulking, and no way was she going to come to Amelia's rescue by speaking now. Daisy might not have noticed the silence, or for all Amelia knew, she might have been worrying where she could fill a prescription, which left Leo to get the conversation started again.

'Three by two. Pequeño,' Leo said, butchering the word. 'How many people live here full time?'

'Inhabitants wise we're a little thin on the ground. There is the community of three artists, the guru and his muse, Sawubona and Tantriana, and, as I said, our *farero*, Pau, lives and works from the lighthouse.'

Maud, who had been silent since her last harumph, harumphed again. It seemed Amelia was to be punished for her desertion.

Yet, she yearned to ask how things were going. Was Maud treating Wendy gently? But if she asked, Maud would sense weakness and attack. Amelia was too vulnerable today; the boulder was too firmly lodged in her stomach to open herself up to Maud's vitriol. So, instead, she chattered on about the island's inhabitants.

'The artists include Beatrice Besson, who makes the most wonderful mosaics—I can't wait for you to see her artwork in the shrine room. Barron is renowned throughout the world for his ornithological impressionism, and he moved here to commune with our flamingos. And then we have our shadow artist, who does not use a name, considers it too plebian. Oliver calls him Hank, after Hank Marvin in the Shadows, but I can't promise he'll answer to it. Other than that, the only inhabitants here are two dozen goats that graze the hillsides, my dogs, Chesterfield and Tulip, and our miraculous flamboyance of flamingos.'

'Can we get any closer to the flamingos?' Leo asked.

'After lunch,' Amelia said. 'We're going to limber up with a yoga class at three-thirty and then jump in the Land Cruiser, or walk up the mountain if you are game, for sundowners and birdwatching.'

She swung the car right, driving through the traditional olivewood gates and into the hotel grounds.

'Oh good,' Amelia said with feeling. 'We've arrived.'

As Amelia pulled up to a stop in the central courtyard, metres from the hotel entrance, she noticed that Oliver had already deposited his charges at the hotel entrance and was busy unloading their luggage from the back of his Land Cruiser.

What she hadn't expected to see was David and Pau standing chest to chest, in the shade of one of the palm trees, gesticulating angrily. Seeing it, and already having had her nerves frayed on the journey from the jetty, Amelia had an urge to stomp over there and tell them to stop making her life more difficult.

Instead, because being the perfect hostess was the order of the day, Amelia gestured impatiently for David to join them and leave her usually perfectly collected Pau in peace.

David just smiled, but she knew Pau had noticed her discomfort when he crossed his arms over his puffed-up chest and snarled, 'I don't believe you. You know nothing about engines!' then stalked off.

David rolled his eyes, mouthed the words, *'fiery Mediterranean bastard,'* shoved his hands in his pockets, and slouched over to greet them.

Embarrassed, Amelia turned to her guests, ready to introduce the perfectly relaxed, smiling David.

But they had all stopped moving. She wasn't sure they were even breathing, and their faces had changed colours to a variety of unhealthy-looking shades.

Not again! What have I done now? she thought, scanning her memory of the past few moments. Nothing.

But there they were. Daisy, her face way beyond its previous pale, was looking *through* David as if he wasn't even there. Maud was rigid, frozen in time, her head tilted to one side with her trademark frown growing on her face. Wendy, standing near the front door, partly hidden under a pile of Maud's assorted possessions, was gaping, eyes like saucers, in the same direction as Maud. Close to Wendy, on the other side of the doorway, was Herb, camera aimed unwaveringly at David. Price was scowling at Daisy, and Leo's face had gone beet red. He was staring determinedly at his shoes, but she knew Leo; he was friendly, relaxed, twinkly. He did not stare at his own shoes. Something had happened. *What the devil did I miss?*

'Ah, um...as you can see, the hotel has been designed so that all the rooms have either sea or mountain views. Daisy and Maud's have both. When you are ready, follow me, and I will show you to your rooms,' Amelia said, turning to lead her guests across the courtyard to the hotel entrance. She felt the stir of air at her back as her guests made to follow her. All the same, she glanced over her shoulder just to be certain, and when she did her eyes caught on Leo.

Maud, Wendy, Daisy, even Price, were all following along behind her, but Leo...Leo had shifted his eyes from the earth at his feet and was glaring daggers into David's back as he sauntered away.

CHAPTER THREE

As Amelia hurried across the hotel lobby, the ceiling-mounted fans circled like vultures over the guests' heads, stirring up welcome gusts of cool air after the blistering afternoon heat.

Oliver grinned at her from behind the reception desk, tossing her once beautifully organised room keys high into the air like an inept juggler at Butterfinger's Circus. Amelia was going to have to deal with Oliver before his unbridled resentment towards her guests sabotaged their ultimate goal.

'Drop the keys, Oliver,' she growled, 'or I will be forced to withdraw your bridge privileges.' Oliver scowled. With just the two of them, he hadn't had the chance to thrash anyone new at bridge for over a year. Which was why, after a visible internal struggle, he surrendered, dropping the keys with a thud and no doubt scarring the surface of her polished, olivewood desk.

Maud was standing halfway between the desk and the drawing room door, slightly apart from the main group. Her body was rigidly upright, her face pinched, lip curled, eyes darting around the room in a way that reminded Amelia of a cobra rearing up to strike. Amelia's own shoulders tensed at the sight, and her body went rigid in readiness for Maud's habitual knee-jerk derision toward any of Amelia's achievements. There was nothing she could do to stop that particular juggernaut; not without tipping the inexplicably tense atmosphere over the edge.

Oliver's scowl deepened, his sharp eyes fixed on her mother. 'Delightful, isn't it?' he purred, stirring the tension just as the fans stirred the air above them.

A battle raged across Maud's face before miraculously settling into a frozen mask of truce. 'Why of course it is. I would expect nothing less from any daughter of mine,' she replied, her tone stiff and formal, her gaze still roaming the room. 'But I cannot imagine why we have not been offered refreshments in this oppressive heat,' she complained, heading toward the stained-glass double doors that led to the airy drawing room.

So, not a truce exactly, Amelia thought, absorbing the impact of that not-so-subtle dig at her lack of hospitality. *And so, it begins...* Amelia watched her mother cross through the threshold, then pictured her making a B-line for the decanters.

Maud was beyond horrified, that much was clear from her frozen mask, which reminded Amelia of the creepy African voodoo mask her father had brought home for her when she was just seven; a treasure from one of his adventures. A mask that Amelia had instantly adored but which had soon been relegated to the basement by a terrified Maud.

But her mother had not spoken a single derisive word about Amelia's hotel, which meant one thing: Maud wanted something from someone, likely Amelia, and she wanted it enough to play nicely with others.

Whatever it was, Amelia would not be giving it to Maud until *after* Saturday's party, if she gave it to her at all. Because everything had fallen into place, hadn't it? Leo and Daisy were here, the hotel—despite whatever Maud might think—*was* beautiful, and now they just had to make it to Saturday's gala where Alfred Boustred would be waiting to sign over the island...or take it from her forever.

What if that monster Price convinces Daisy to leave? Or what if after I explain Maud's betrayal, Leo decides he can't stay on the island with her? Everything will have been for nothing!

I should lock them in their bloody rooms...

No, Amelia had invited them early for two reasons.

First, she wanted to reconnect with her old friends, mend old wounds, and maybe even create some new memories. If she wanted El Pedrusco to be a raving success, who better than her old friends to help her? Three musketeers were better than one.

And second, it would leave her two days before the big party to track them down, persuade, cajole or, heaven forbid, manipulate them into doing the right thing.

But now she realised it gave Maud time to ruin everything. She had a habit of doing that.

Suddenly, the idea of locking everyone in their rooms didn't sound so insane.

Oliver cleared his throat, gently reminding Amelia that she was ignoring her other guests. She was making Maud the centre of her universe, *again*.

Unfreezing, she moved to sort through the messy pile of keys, grabbing the three she needed before saying, 'The hotel staff, including our chef, Jordi, have headed back to Mallorca with the yacht. They're taking a few days off, which leaves Oliver and me in charge of your comfort. But fear not, Oliver is a very capable cook and if you are in need of nourishment between meals, there is always fresh fruit and homemade cookies, as well as a variety of juices and tea and coffee in your rooms and in the dining room. So, you won't starve, and the professionals will be returning in good time to prepare for the grand opening on Saturday,' Amelia said with an airy smile that did not reach her eyes. They were eyes that still longed to follow her mother into the drawing room.

'I'll show Daisy, Price, and Leo up to their rooms,' Amelia said to Oliver, holding the keys like prizes over her head. 'If you wouldn't mind grabbing Maud and showing her to her suite before we lay out the lunch buffet in the dining room.' Then, raising her voice for everyone to hear, she continued her tour guide impersonation. 'We have an hour of free time now, so that you can rest, freshen up, and help yourself to the lunch buffet. Afterwards, we will go down to the shrine room for yoga and meditation. Finally, we will head straight up La Colina Alta for a nice cuppa and a closer look at our splendid flamingo visitors.

'Herb,' she said, twisting around, searching for the journalist, meaning to give him directions to his bungalow. But he was gone.

'Like the bloodhound journalist he is,' Leo said, his voice an impersonation of a David Attenborough nature documentary. 'Herb Hogan has stalked his prey to the drawing room where he and his fellow predator will be rewarded with three fingers of scotch and a cube of ice.'

Amelia's own imagination conjured a more likely scene of Maud guzzling directly from the decanter, and Herb riffling through the cupboards in search of a juicy story. She winced at the thought. 'Oh-kaaaay... If you would please follow your allocated host, we can all leave the...predators...to enjoy their kill.'

'Watch your step on these stairs,' Amelia warned as she took hold of the handrail and began to climb. Left foot to step one, right foot to step two, then back to left for step three, and right four. *Left odds, right evens...always.* There were twenty-one steps from ground to first floor. Starting with left and ending with left. *Symmetry.* She drew in the deepest breath her lungs could muster, then let it out slowly.

'Did you know that one person falls down the stairs every 90 seconds in England? Probably far more here in Spain with all the marble floors and industrious mopping that goes on,' she joked as she led her charges up the helical staircase. Leo, Daisy, and Price trailed up behind her and then followed as she walked toward the wide corridor that led to the East Wing.

'No elevator,' Price gasped as he lumbered along in her wake. Amelia hesitated long enough to glance over her shoulder to see him mounting the final step at the head of the staircase. He was shimmering like a mirage, his dove-grey shirt turned charcoal with sweat.

Amelia threw Daisy a conspiratorial grin, but Daisy was still an empty shell, apparently inhabiting a dream world where no one could touch her.

'This one's yours, Leo,' Amelia said, unlocking the door to his suite and pushing it wide open.

The room was furnished in dark wood, with three soft-yellow walls, and the fourth wall decorated with turquoise patterned wallpaper behind the canopied bed.

'Rest, freshen up, partake of the buffet, but be sure to be down in the lobby at three-thirty prompt,' she ordered with a smile. Leo tugged on his forelock and bowed low, before disappearing behind the door.

The next two doors were opposite one another. 'Price, this is yours,' she said swinging the door open. 'Oh...and the lift is tucked away just around the corner at the end of the corridor in case you need it.'

'Only works in one direction, does it?' Price practically snarled in response. Amelia cringed; they should have taken it on the way up.

Damn it, Amelia! Can't you do anything right?! her internalised version of her mother's voice raged inside her head. She heard it so often that she'd even given it a name: Inner-Maud.

Before she could apologise, Price disappeared behind his door.

'Don't mind him,' Daisy said, her first spontaneous words since her arrival. 'It's not personal. He can't abide anyone.'

'Like Maud,' Amelia murmured, opening the door to Daisy's suite and ushering her through.

Daisy walked directly into the centre of the room and spun in a slow circle. Amelia watched as she took in the white painted walls and ceiling, the fine wicker furniture, and the palm print curtains and bedcovers.

'It's lovely,' she said. Her words sounded to Amelia like those of a polite child thanking a distant aunt for an unwelcome Christmas or birthday gift—perhaps a monogrammed handkerchief—as she drifted across the room to stand by the floor-to-ceiling window overlooking the beach. The window was half open, and a disharmony of gulls screamed abuse at each other overhead.

Amelia was about to launch into more proud-mamma descriptions of the island when Daisy slammed the window shut, locking it tight, then began checking all the other locks, moving from one window to the next, rattling the catches then moving to the next. She flicked every light switch on, then off; she clicked the torch on and off. She even struck a match, then counted how many were left in the box. This all happened while Amelia stood rooted to her spot just inside the doorway. Not for the first time that afternoon, she thought, *Thank goodness she's here. If anywhere can heal whatever is wrong with my old friend, it is El Pedrusco.*

'Are you alright?' she asked. In days gone by, she would have rushed across the room and hugged her tight. But this was now, and so much had changed between them.

'Why wouldn't I be?' Daisy asked vaguely.

'Well...uh...I'm not a great fan of the dark either, but...' she left the final words hanging, choosing instead to gesture first toward the windows and then to the blackened match on the dresser.

'Oh that,' Daisy said, a twang in her voice she had not possessed when they were two little English girls playing Nancy Drew to Leo's black-hearted robber. 'I'm better, or at least I am when I'm home in LA,' Daisy explained, though her jaw was clenched, and her eyes were glued to the window that overlooked the driveway. 'It was years before I could sleep more than an hour at one time, but now I can. It's just...I need to know I'm safe.'

'You should have come home!' The words burst out of Amelia. 'We could have helped. You know Seb and I would have done anything to help. I wrote and I called and called but you never answered. I wanted to be there for you, but you didn't let me in!' Amelia's voice broke from years of pent-up emotion she had never acknowledged, even to herself.

Daisy watched her outburst with impassive eyes. 'What use would it have been? What use to drag you down with me?'

'I could have listened—'

'And what, pray tell, would I have said? Perhaps I could have told you about the terrorised girl, kept caged like an animal, bruised and broken for the entertainment of monsters?' Amelia gasped in horror at the words. 'Yes, now you see. I had enough nightmares of my own without being responsible for *yours*.' Daisy's voice rose on every word to a snarling, feral crescendo. It was horrible to witness, but it was real and it was honest and it was *present*.

In that moment, Daisy was more animated—more *alive*—than she had been for the previous hour. Perhaps there was still hope for her old friend.

The door swung open, and Price barged through it. 'The sarcastic innkeeper delivered your garment bag along with my luggage,' he said. 'It will need pressing before the damned party. Do you want me to take it down to the laundry?'

'Don't bother, Peppy. It can wait,' Daisy replied, taking the transparent garment bag from him and hanging the shimmering indigo evening gown in the wardrobe.

You'd have to be stupid to believe this charade, Amelia thought. A sudden interest in the laundering of party dresses? Had Price bounded in on his white charger in defence of his client?

Perhaps. But Amelia was going to allow the charade to pass without comment. He was, after all, looking out for her, even if Amelia had wished he hadn't. They'd been getting somewhere.

Having achieved his goal, EveryoneHasTheirPrice Whitney spun on his heel with surprising grace for a big man and made to leave.

'Don't forget our yoga and meditation class at three-thirty!' Daisy called after him, a weak smile plastered on her face. There was genuine friendship between the two, and even though Amelia was certain she could never warm to that kind of rude, Amelia was happy that her friend had found him in the snake pit that was Hollywood.

Price poked his head back round the door. 'You won't find Price Whitney twisting himself into a pretzel, not even for Hollywood's favourite princess. I'm gonna fly solo and take myself off on a tour of your itty-bitty island, see if I can't regain my land legs.'

With that he peered at Daisy, like he had X-ray vision and was scanning her for...well, Amelia wasn't quite sure, but she thought perhaps he was scanning her for wounds. Then, after a painful fifteen or so seconds, the peer turned into a scowl as he wrapped his sausage fingers around the back of his neck and rubbed back and forth. He shook his head, muttering, 'I knew this was a bad idea.' Then he left.

Daisy was back in the centre of the room looking like a lost child. Not knowing what else to do, the boulder growing exponentially in her stomach, Amelia turned to leave.

She thought she might have spotted a chink in her friend's armour, but she could also tell she would get no further just now. Still, Amelia decided, she was going to make the most of the next few days. *Everything is cracked...that's how the light gets in*, she thought, bodging a recent Leonard Cohen lyric as she took hold of the handle and pressed downward.

'It really *is* a lovely room,' Daisy said, her voice barely a whisper. 'And thank you for the furniture. I'll make sure to be down in the lobby in good time.'

Amelia nodded. Much of the wicker furniture—the rocking chair, the old cabinet, the sideboard that now doubled as a dresser—was from Uncle Seb's drawing room in the old house. Amelia had commissioned the bed and the dressing tables to match. She had missed her old friend and she had gone to great lengths to make her feel comfortable.

But even though she'd given that gift to Daisy, she'd made certain to hold back the most important piece, his writing desk. It held such fond memories—her sitting perched on extra cushions beside him while he worked on some project or other, and she drew pictures of the palm trees she could see out of the window—that she could not bear to part with it. *That* now had pride of place in her own suite, although Pau had painted it white to match the rest of the furnishings and it doubled up as a dressing table.

'I'll see you later,' Amelia said, turning to look at her friend. 'Oh, and Daisy?'

'Yes Amelia?' Daisy replied, her face stiff with tension, her voice strained. She'd had enough for one day.

'Welcome home.'

Amelia was peeking out between the gap in her thighs. Her legs were spread wide, her knees locked, her upper body collapsed forward and she 'swayed like a tree in the wind,' according to Sawubona, who was sitting cross-legged with his palms together in prayer position, chanting, 'Oh my, how big is your bum?' over and over. At least that was what it sounded like to Amelia. *If this is meant to be boosting my minuscule self-esteem, it is not working.*

Daisy was lying like a pile of sharpened sticks on the mat, while Maud stood upright, impatiently tapping one sock-covered foot on the floor. Leo and Wendy were gamely trying to follow Sawubona's instructions, and Herb was sitting on his bum, collapsed like a wobbly toddler, while Sawubona droned on, 'Oh my, how big is your bum? Oh my, how big is your bum?'

Gazing between the gap in her thighs, silently reminiscing about everything she loved about standing upright, and wondering whether, at this stage, she was even capable of such a feat, Amelia spotted Beatrice Besson by the door. She watched as the mosaic artist glided gracefully into the room, a lovely orange and green cereal-sized mosaic bowl in her hands complimenting her green smock and her hair which was one shade lighter than the orange of the offering. *Like a living benediction,* Amelia thought. *But it might just be the rush of blood to my head.*

The room filled with the scent of bougainvillea flowers as Beatrice deposited her offering on the shrine. Amelia gave a little wave of one hand between her legs. It put her off-balance and she tipped too far forward, falling, but she improvised, turning it into a forward roll like they'd practiced in school gym class. Unfortunately, Amelia had never really mastered that particular roll, and she ended up sprawled on her mat, looking like a more crumpled, curvier version of Daisy's stick-pile.

Her head was spinning. Her body rebelled and she retched, and by the time Amelia untangled herself, Beatrice had completed her little bow or curtsy or whatever it was she did on her daily visits and glided out the door.

Amelia focused on righting herself, then scanned the room, checking that none of her guests were similarly indisposed. Leo the contortionist threw her a wink, silently confirming he had witnessed her humiliation, while Wendy was bravely persevering with the class. Maud, unsurprisingly, was still tapping her toes, but Herb and Daisy appeared to have picked up their mats and walked, like in the scriptures. The pinched look on Maud's face told Amelia she had missed something significant. But what?

Oh well, maybe Friday's tantra class will be more to their liking, Amelia thought, crossing her fingers while reluctantly opening her legs and collapsing forward once again.

Fifteen minutes later, after making shapes with her body it was not genetically intended to make, Sawubona had stopped his incessant chanting.

Ten minutes after that, Amelia stood with Maud, Price, Leo, and Wendy outside the front of the shrine room, waiting for Oliver to bring the Land Cruiser around. She had taken a moment to pop to the kitchen, which is where her hounds, Chessie and

Tulip, could predictably be found whenever she lost sight of them.

The guests would have the choice of riding in the Land Cruiser up the unmade road to the summit or hiking there with Amelia and the dogs.

Just as the Land Cruiser rolled to a halt, Daisy appeared from behind the hotel, walking from an area where the cliffs were as high as skyscrapers—still wearing those blasted stiletto heels—and Herb strolled up from his bungalow, which was just to the east of the main building, nestled at the foot of La Colina and set well back from the cliffs.

'Please do be careful if you go walking along the clifftops, especially in those shoes,' Amelia said, her voice tight with worry. 'You do know that a whole gaggle of girls have died after falling off their platform shoes?'

'Yes Lia, I have heard the tales. Though, in my defence, those poor sweet babies had not been walking on spikes for almost two decades. And if I do happen to fall, I pinkie-swear not to sue you from beyond the grave,' Daisy replied, pursing her lips, spinning ever so competently on said heels, and marched across to the Land Cruiser like a farmer in wellies. She pulled up her dress, just enough that she could raise her foot twelve inches off the ground to reach the sill and hopped gracefully up onto the front of the two rows of bench seats behind the driver.

Amelia hoped the sarcasm was a sign the island was already weaving its magic and healing the trauma Daisy so obviously still carried. She then watched as Maud, Wendy, and Price all hopped into the Land Cruiser after her.

'Looks like it's just you, me, and the dogs taking a hike, old duck,' Leo said from beside her. His voice was like a warm hug, and she found herself turning to him and grinning.

'That's good. Because I owe you an explanation and an apology, and no doubt it'll come out smoother without an audience,' she said as the Land Cruiser took off down the driveway with Oliver honking the horn like a goose on crack.

'Sounds deep, Lia... But whatever it is you think warrants an apology, to me it's water under the bridge. Everything is good between us,' Leo said, heading off after the Land Cruiser.

'*Ahem.*' Amelia cleared her throat to attract his attention, then instead of following him down the driveway, she walked across the front of the hotel building, past the eastern bungalows and along the dirt track that led up the mountain. Leo followed. Ahead, they could see the dirt thrown up by the Land Cruiser's wheels as Oliver turned left off the main road and onto a track on the far side of La Colina Alta.

'I love the fact you forgive so easily, and I'll definitely be taking you up on that, but all the same, I would like the opportunity to explain what happened seven years ago.'

'It's your choice if you want to dig up ancient history, my love,' Leo said. Then, as she was about to launch into said explanation, she was sure she heard him mutter, 'Our history is the least of my worries.' Amelia felt a shiver roll up her spine as she remembered Leo's stare boring into David's back from earlier. She wanted to ask him about it, but first she needed to bare her soul.

'As you know, I was eight years old when I lost my father. What you may not know, but I'm sure you guessed, over the next few years I slowly, inch by inch, lost what was left of my mother to the bitter demon inside her. At fifteen, I lost my best friend Daisy, and at twenty-three, I lost you. After those hits, I had only one person left in this world who was more precious to me than life, apart from grumpy old Oliver, and that was my Uncle Seb. When I lost him a year ago, I had nothing left, nothing at all.

'And the strange thing is, after the initial shock and grief, I slowly discovered that at last I was free. I had nothing left to lose and so the fear I carried with me wherever I went just slipped away one day, never to return.' Leo was smiling, his teeth gleaming in the sunlight. Though he looked sceptical.

'Oh, don't worry too much. Caution is a habit that does not let go so easily. I suspect I will always project my fears onto those I love...' she didn't finish that thought; just went back to the story she was desperate to recount.

'Seven years ago, before you went off in search of both our fathers, you had a meeting with Maud, correct?' she asked, grabbing for Tulip's collar as she went barrelling past them and into the undergrowth. *Damn, it looks like I'm going to be hosing her off later.*

'I did,' Leo replied, then...nothing. It seemed if she wanted to apologise, it would be her doing all the talking.

'She told you I felt sorry for you. "After all, dear Leopold, you were effectively orphaned when your father went missing,"' Amelia said, imitating Maud's nasal tones. 'She told you that I only cared about you because of our shared loss. That I had voiced my trepidation at being tied to you. But Leo, she lied.' Amelia dragged in a lungful of air as she skirted a wide crack in the path, and continued.

'I knew from the age of five, hiding just off stage at one of Maud's productions, that I was destined to marry a handsome prince. I wasn't fussy about him actually having royal blood flowing through his veins. Even at five, that part wasn't important. What was important was that he'd simply *adore* me from our first chance meeting on Piccadilly, until the day he died peacefully in his sleep, of a broken heart, just months after I had passed away from a short, and hopefully painless, illness. And the important part of *that* was that he died *after* me so I wouldn't have to suffer through losing him.' Leo smirked the old Leo smirk, amused. He held out his hand to help her clamber over some rocks that barred the narrow path. She didn't judge his smirk, for he had heard the story many times before.

'I embellished the dream through the years. We would live behind a white picket fence in a tiny village in the Cotswolds or the Lake District or some other romantic sounding corner of England, and I would fill our house with shiny-faced children who'd attend the local Church of England school where they'd excel, or not, because *that* wouldn't matter, as long as they were healthy and happy.'

'Then, at seven years old, I met a darling boy of nine named Leopold Alcott. I had a face for my prince.' This time Leo grinned, then let out a shrill whistle calling Chessie back from the brow of a small rise in front of them. The dog stopped and looked over his shoulder before lolloping off into the undergrowth in search of *his* great love, Tulip.

'Through the years, I crushed on you terribly, and when at eighteen you asked me on a date, I thought I had died and gone to Heaven. I jumped at the chance, of course, and after that, if we hadn't already been joined at the hip, we would have been then.

'You were my first,' she said quietly, and Leo flushed beetroot. 'Leo and Lia forever, it seemed so perfect. I shared my dreams with you, and you shared yours with me.

'Everything was wonderful. I was in love. But then, something happened. I couldn't understand it. On the day I was certain you were going to ask me that biggest of all questions, you stood me up. Days went by and nothing.

'I had not woken up in my long dreamed of fairy tale with a sparkling ring on my finger, but in The Critical World of Maud Lavender. The familiar recrimination-filled world I had inhabited my entire life.

'Then a letter dropped on the mat four days later. You told me you were off to Africa in search of my father, Maynard, and your father, Bennet, and you would not return until you located them. I knew then that you had got cold feet. That I was not enough; not the dream girl to you like you were the dream boy to me.

'So, I let go of that dream of caterwauling children, hungry for their breakfasts and late for the school bus, in Market Lavenham or Stockley Chippenham or some other double-barrelled village that should have been mine.'

Somehow, they had come to a halt. Leo's attention was full on her as he stood facing her, reaching out to take hold of both her hands.

'Lia...' That one word was a plea, a plea to stop torturing herself.

'Then, thirteen months ago, after years of agony, when I was certain the scab had healed over that wound, I learned that Maud had caused my pain. And what was more, she had not an ounce of shame over it.

'She had gone to visit you, and she had told you not the truth she claimed, but a horrible, terrible lie. And instead of coming to me, *talking to me*, you left.'

'Calm down, Lia—' Leo tried again to stop the diatribe. It *had* been a very long time, but Amelia was a woman possessed, purging the black tar that had infested her soul for more than half a decade.

'I have lived in fear for as long as I can remember. Most of it was Maud's fear, carried by me. But some of it is mine. The part that is mine is the part that grew from knowing what it felt like to reach out for your dream, to want it so badly you can hardly breathe, and then lose it. To lose the person you love. That part, not wanting to take a chance again after falling so hard...that was all mine.

'Then Uncle Seb's gift allowed to me to escape her. I can barely remember those first weeks after I arrived on El Pedrusco. I only left my room to shower and eat. But soon the island sun tempted me to the beach, then to exploring, reacquainting myself with the old haunts I remembered from our childhood adventures. How we had searched every nook, cranny, and cave on the island for the heaps of Christmas gifts we knew Uncle Seb—anti-grinch that he was—bought for us.'

'And the clifftop cairns we built and maintained,' Leo added. 'I still do that when I'm hiking, you know.'

'Me too,' Amelia said, picking up a rock and studying the white lines that bisected it. 'It took a while, but soon I found myself clambering up rocky outcrops, then venturing into those damp caves behind the hidden beach and roaming the laterite paths along the clifftops in search of those cairns. As I explored, my heart slowly healed, at least a little, which allowed me to at last fully understand Uncle Seb's dream of opening a healing hotel on this island. It was like an epiphany. If this place could heal my own wounded heart, couldn't it surely do the same for others?'

'This is your new beginning,' Leo murmured, the light of understanding illuminating his face.

'Yes, a new beginning. A different dream. But a dream nonetheless.'

'And Seb really wanted me here as a last dying wish?'

Amelia hesitated. *No, I've come this far with him.*

'Leo... Uncle set me a deathbed challenge, and part of that was to bring you here. I can't begin to understand his motives other than that they were guided by his innate goodness.'

Leo's mouth turned down. 'Lia—'

'I know, I'm sorry I wasn't a hundred percent honest. But it was all in a good cause, and I want you to know that I would have wanted you here anyway, wanted it right down to the marrow in my bones. I needed this opportunity to make sure you knew—right down to the marrow in *your* bones—that the feelings I had for you back then were not pity, they were love. But mostly I just wanted you here because...I missed you.'

There they stood, two minutes from the top of her almost-mountain. Amelia facing Leo, both her hands wrapped in his. Staring into each other's eyes, hers green, his bright blue, and slowly, tentatively, they began to smile.

'The course of true love never did run smooth,' Amelia muttered.

'*A Midsummer Night's Dream*,' Leo said. 'You do love to quote Shakespeare at me, don't you? And where the devil is Puck to lighten the mood when you need him?' he asked, laughing, before his face grew serious.

'Thank you, Lia,' Leo said. 'I've missed you too. Thank you for bringing me here and for explaining. It means a lot to me that you want me here. This year has been tough, and it feels good to be here in a place where I have only happy memories.'

Amelia nodded. 'So, what happened?'

Leo paused, swallowed, and then said, 'You know what a dunce I can be, right? How gullible?' Amelia's lips turned upward into a smirk.

Oh yes, her Leo had a massive heart and he certainly led with it, sometimes when he should have been guarding it.

'Well, I got mixed up with someone I shouldn't have, and like a fool, I got my pals in London mixed up with this can't lose venture he introduced me to. And that venture turned out to be a tad...*irregular*, which means I've become a bit of a persona non grata in dear old Blighty.'

'Go on. What happened?'

Leo shrugged, and gave a half laugh that didn't look natural. 'No need to get into the details. Suffice to say, it all blew up just before your last letter... So, I thought, "Leo, old man, now would be a fantastic time to take a little holiday with old chums to give everyone a little time for the dust to settle.' Amelia's glow faded a little and she felt the air being sucked out of her lungs when she realised he hadn't come for her; at least not in the way she would have liked.

But of course, Leo hadn't. Why would he have when he thought Amelia had never truly cared for him?

'Anyway,' he continued. 'Thank you for telling me the truth and thank you for giving me a place to stay. It might help me sort out my head.'

Amelia nodded and smiled, okay with ending their talk there. There would be opportunities to speak later, she knew, and at least the weight of her apology had been lifted off her shoulders. She had done it. She had cleared the wreckage, and she was ready for whatever came next.

'Shall we catch up to the others. I don't know about you, but I could murder a martini,' Amelia said. Leopold Alcott nodded and dragged her the rest of the way up to the peak.

CHAPTER FOUR

Leo hurdled the final boulder, then took hold of Amelia's hand and hoisted her up and over it too. Tulip and Chessie were gambolling at their heels. Tulip had something brown and nasty clenched between her teeth as she played a game of tag with Chessie.

Oh well. It wasn't as if Tulip didn't find something fetid and rotten on almost every walk they took. Thank goodness for the garden hose between here and Amelia's white cotton sheets.

Elated, Amelia couldn't resist quoting, 'Made it, Ma! Top of the World!'

Leo grinned. 'James Cagney in *White Heat?*' he asked.

Amelia nodded, grinning. 'Let's hope there'll be no bullets up here.'

As they emerged from the windswept thicket of thorny shrubs, Amelia was pleased to see that Oliver was playing the perfect host. Some of her guests were sipping on perfectly chilled drinks he had ferried up in cold boxes, others had dainty porcelain teacups with saucers balanced on their palms, and all were staring down through binoculars at the magical pinkness of the Greater Flamingos.

Amelia strode across to the old ammunition box Oliver had packed the binoculars in and removed a set for herself and another for Leo. She pulled him to an empty spot behind the railing she'd had installed before opening the island to the public. *Safety first!* her inner Girl Guide whispered, reminding her of the cautionary tale of Mary Williams and the Singed Eyebrows.

'How many are left this late in the season?' Leo asked, using his binoculars to point at the scattering of wading birds below.

'There were close to fifty when the season was in full swing, and almost thirty have made the island their home,' Amelia said. 'The majority of the Balearic population spend their winters in Mallorca or one of the other larger islands. There's more food. But we have some diehard fans drawn here like alkies to a free bar. They can live for up to forty years, and are now bringing their children with them, so our little group is on the rise.'

'They sure are a sight to see,' Price interrupted, peering through his binoculars as he dabbed his sweating forehead with a facecloth he'd pilfered from his suite. 'Will we have a chance to shoot a couple while we are here? Maybe we could—' Amelia's horror-filled face stopped the next words on the tip of his tongue.

'Absolutely not!' she screeched. 'It's against the law!' Not that she knew that for a fact. It was likely only Oliver knew whether it was indeed against Spanish law to hunt flamingos. But it didn't matter. This was *her* island, and if it wasn't against Spanish law, it most certainly was against El Pedrusco law.

'It would just be one. What would be the harm in it?'

'They mate for life! They are gregarious creatures; they couple up, then breed at the same time as their friends so all the kids can grow up together. So, when one dies, it's really two plus all the offspring they could have produced.' Price took a slug of his San Miguel not looking impressed by her tale of flamingo amigos. His brows furrowed and Amelia tensed for his next words.

'What about the goats?' he asked. 'We passed a whole bunch on the way up here. A couple of them looked lame...one was missing an eye. You can't say one of those dud ones would be missed!'

'No! Absolutely not! No hunting on the island. No fishing, no crossbows, no trapping, and absolutely no shooting,' Amelia spat out, her voice rising as she remembered how dear old Uncle Seb had nursed those duds. *'Never leave a man behind,'* he had told her, and she wasn't about to go against him on that.

'In fact, new rule. No guns allowed on any part of this island,' Amelia said in a way that could not be misconstrued. There began her proclamation. 'Guns are dangerous; without any redeeming qualities. So, it is with great joy that I now declare this island a gun-free zone.' By the time she finished speaking, Amelia was panting, her limbs rigid with indignation. Glancing at the faces around her, she realised her aversion to Price and his murderous ideas were a tad heavy on drama.

Only Herb wasn't staring at her. Instead, he had his binoculars—no, his telephoto lens—firmly trained on one of three ledges beneath them. Amelia raised her own binoculars, shifting them in the direction Herb's camera was pointing.

Though she knew his fascination wasn't with the flamingos, Amelia still gasped at what he had his camera lens trained on. Beneath them, on the rock platform, Sawubona and Tantriana were practicing a complicated—no...*impossible*—tantric ritual. Naked.

'Get away from there,' Amelia hissed, rushing across to Herb, making sure to stay well back from the railing. She grabbed his camera from his sweaty grip.

'Give them a little privacy, old boy,' Leo drawled, taking the camera from Amelia's shaking hands and passing it to Oliver.

They had an audience. Only Daisy was still looking out over the lake, towards the harbour. She was watching David as he sat on a chair under an awning on the deck of his boat. He had his old briefcase open on the floor beside him. Daisy's eyes were hidden behind her sunglasses, but her brow was furrowed, head cocked to one side, and she was so still Amelia could have sworn she wasn't breathing. *What on earth?*

David must have sensed their eyes peering down at him, because he looked up at their little group, spotted Amelia and smiled his wolfish mushy pea smile, before taking off his ridiculous captain's hat and waving it around in a wide arc over his head.

Amelia waved back with a lot less enthusiasm, then turned back to Daisy, who was now slumped on a nearby rock. Amelia approached and sat down beside her.

'Are you okay?' she asked.

'Yes. I think so,' Daisy replied, clearing her throat. 'It's just that it feels strange being back here. Surreal. Every stranger I see looks like the boogieman. Something about the day feels...ominous. I don't know...'

Amelia remained silent, giving her old friend space to share if she needed to.

Daisy took a deep breath. 'I haven't had flashbacks of the kidnapping for a long time. Not until today. I can't quite put my finger on it, but something about this place, or maybe these people, has brought it all back.' Daisy shivered and Amelia grabbed hold of her hand and squeezed. She could feel every single bone in that hand. *A strong tramontana wind would blow my fragile friend away.*

'Let's go back,' Amelia suggested, climbing to her feet and dragging her friend away from the edge, towards the group.

Price was back at the Land Cruiser, as was a chastened looking Herb. Oliver had the disgruntled man's camera clutched in his hands and spoke to him in a stern voice. 'You will have it back in time for this evening's festivities, but only if you promise not to make more of a nuisance of yourself than is entirely necessary.'

'It's a funny thing,' Herb said, smirking like an unrepentant child caught with his hand in the cookie jar. 'How you toffs practically beg me to attend your stick-up-your-own-arse self-congratulatory-soiree, but once I'm here, doing my bloody job, you moan and groan about respecting your privacy. Hypocrites,' he said as he stomped off.

Wendy was packing the cold box away and Maud and Leo were having a heated discussion. Amelia guessed Leo was confronting her mother over the events Amelia had revealed on their walk.

'Maud, be careful so close to the edge,' Amelia called to her mother, just as the ground slipped from beneath her mother's foot. Her face froze, her arms flailed around like she was trying to fly, and

Amelia's heart skipped at least one beat. But Leo shot out one hand and grabbed hold of Maud's shoulder, dragging her away from the edge.

'This conversation isn't over,' Maud hissed after collecting herself. Without a word of thanks, she stalked back to the Land Cruiser.

The journey down was far quicker, partly because gravity was kind, but also because after she waved off her guests, the spectre of her mother appeared out of the dust kicked up by the Land Cruiser.

Amelia, who had been enjoying the reprieve of Maud's loaded silences, was not ready for battle to recommence, so she turned toward the path and made her escape down the rocky descent. The awkward run-walk she adopted quickly became a slow jog, then a faster one until eventually she was running full pelt, as if fleeing a pack of wild hyaenas, and instigating countermeasures to evade her determined mother cantering after her and calling out her name in an accidental imitation of a braying donkey.

She still hadn't managed to put much distance between them, when she stubbed her toe on a rock, then attempted evasive manoeuvres before taking an unladylike flight. She reached out her arms to save herself, which only served to cause her to stumble around like a drunken sailor—a trip to the hospital in Mallorca flashed in front of her eyes—and she bounced off a nearby pine and windmilled backwards before landing on her bum in the dirt. Amelia's knees and palms stung, as did her eyes.

It couldn't have been more than ten seconds later that Maud was looming over her. She was surprised at her speed.

Amelia stayed where she was, though she shifted her eyes from one of the large orange rocks that littered the landscape to another, and silently counted them—*one, two, three*. It was what she did when she caught herself judging someone, which wasn't exactly often, but it did happen. Then, she did her best to redirect her thoughts to serenity and peace.

Restored, though still panting heavily, Amelia prepared to clamber to her feet and recommence her run when Maud gasped out, 'If you had just *slowed down* for a moment, I could have said the few words I needed to say, and *you* would have avoided an airborne near-death experience. Please be kind enough to stay still for ten seconds so I can do it now, after which I will happily leave you in peace!'

'It feels to me,' Amelia said, 'that you and I have exchanged more than enough words for one lifetime'.

Maud's eyebrows shot up into her hairline. Before the dreaded Will reading, Amelia had disagreed with Maud perhaps five or six times in her entire life. Today, it was looking like her habit of passive compliance was at an end. Amelia found she was enjoying the moment, but she had little practice, while Maud had more than five decades of it.

'Alright,' she continued wearily, prodding one grazed palm with her forefinger. 'Why don't you just spit it out so I can see to my guests.'

'I don't need you to come home,' Maud said. By which Amelia knew she meant to, *come home immediately*. 'Wendy is extraordinary,' Maud added, which translated to, *Wendy doesn't pass muster and is quite ordinary*, which Amelia knew, to Maud, was beyond the pale.

'Is that all?'

'No, that is *not* all. I should have you know, if you're even interested, that the words for my latest play are flowing like the vodka at Café Pushkin. It will be a triumph.' Maud had completed her Pollyanna speech with the greatest lie of them all. It was clear that writer's block had set in.

This did not bode well for Amelia. In fact, it undoubtedly meant that the thing Maud wanted, that Amelia had sensed through her mother's uncharacteristic, almost charitable forbearance, was for Amelia to come home, no questions asked. Maud would spend the coming days relentlessly badgering Amelia, and it would continue after the opening.

Perhaps, Amelia thought in horror, she would go as far as sabotaging Amelia's inheritance.

'Mother...' Amelia tried to stop the flow.

'The one cloud on my horizon is dear Daisy.' Amelia gritted her teeth. Her whole life, Maud had used Daisy's perfection, her suffering, and her celebrity to highlight Amelia's perceived mediocrity. After a year in paradise, Amelia's armour against Maud was brittle through lack of use. She wasn't sure her newfound non-compliance would stand up to a 'Daisy would have made a better daughter than you,' tirade.

'I'm so worried about her. When we were waiting for you for *so long* in the lobby. You know, before that exhibitionist guru traumatised us all with his ugly song and uninvited physical activity.' Amelia winced and balled her fists. 'Daisy told me her time on the island had always felt like a dream, a dream that preceded an unimaginable nightmare...which was of course a nightmare for us all. She went on to explain that this trip will be an ending, an ending she yearns for. Then, when she went walking along the cliffs by the hotel in those sky-high heels, I wondered...'

'Mother!' Amelia gasped.

'I do not mean to frighten you. I only point it out so that nothing terrible happens to get in the way of the party...*and your inheritance*. It would be awful if you were to lose it this late in the day.'

Maud's words sounded like a threat.

Still, her words caused Amelia to drag in a shaky breath. She clambered up to her feet, thinking, *No, I cannot—will not—believe it. There is no way that Daisy, having lived through so much then risen from the ashes to become Hollywood's darling, can be thinking of ending it all. And damn Maud for even suggesting it!*

Amelia, think! She's planting a fearful seed just behind the boulder in the pit of your stomach. But this time, Amelia promised herself, *I am not going to water it so it grows and shuts out the light I have found on this island. I'll kill her before she robs me of that.*

She took off down the hill towards the hotel, leaving her mother behind.

CHAPTER FIVE

Amelia stood at the dining room window, gazing out over the magnificent vista of the hotel gardens, then to the lawns rolling down to the palm tree-lined beach and on over the Mediterranean Sea. She barely noticed the scent of jasmine emanating from the low hedges framing the pool and patio area. She was agitated, which was easily signalled by the staccato tap-tapping of her foot on the marble floor.

That afternoon—after a brief shower necessitated by her unscheduled sprint down the side of La Colina Alta, and a five-minute break sitting on her bed, playing an imaginary tape in her head of Uncle

Seb telling her what a wonderful job she was doing and how the party would be a roaring success—she and Oliver had buried themselves under a pile of papers, heads bowed close together as they pored over the fine details of the upcoming party.

Little did her guests know that they did indeed possess one radio that was just within signal range of Mallorca. They were taking this time to make absolutely sure they had thought of everything so that they could message the staff to bring anything they'd forgotten before they left the big island on Saturday.

Amelia had left Oliver an hour before dinner so she could take another quick shower before changing into her sea-green evening dress that flowed around her like she was wearing scarves tied together. When she had bought it, Maud had told her she looked like a gypsy fortune-teller. But that had done nothing to put her off her new purchase.

After adding some light makeup and an even lighter floral scent, she hurried down to the kitchen to decant the homemade gazpacho soup starter into Uncle Seb's magnificent antique sterling silver soup tureens. It was a simple but necessary dish before the weekend's planned hedonistic gastronomy.

Amelia then laid out the cold buffet and fruit salad, to which she would add the homemade almond-based dessert, made in advance by the chef using almonds from her own trees.

Thinking about all she and Oliver had achieved, Amelia wondered if it wouldn't have been more apt for her to be laying in a darkened room recovering from exhaustion rather than tap-tapping her foot in agitation.

'There you are, my dear,' Oliver called, and she glanced over her shoulder to see him framed in the dining room doorway, the light from the foyer chandeliers reflecting off the stained-glass door to produce dancing prisms of light, darting like fairies around his head. 'Are you ready?'

Amelia had told him all about her mother's strange pursuit after sundowners. Oliver, of course, had found it hilarious and he had continued to burst into gales of laughter every time he'd thought of it as they worked together that afternoon. Which was why his question had deeper meaning than the surface one.

He wanted to know if she was ready to face her mother after Maud lied to her face, and then told her that her once best friend was planning suicide.

'I have laid the table with the bluntest of butter knives and our shortest pronged forks to avoid serious bloodshed,' Amelia assured him.

'Very good,' Oliver said with a smirk. 'It is now precisely eight. Shall I strike the dinner gong?'

'Yes, go ahead,' Amelia replied, turning back to the window for one final look at the tranquil scene. She pulled in a deep fortifying breath, like a warrior donning her armour, at which moment, a dark spectre crossed the sky, blocking out the last orange rays from the dying sun. Amelia squinted, scanning the strangely mobile darkness for one hint of what had happened.

After a few seconds she could make out a mass of swirling wings, then a wall of squawking screeching hit her ears, making her wince, as her entire flock of thirty or so flamingos rose up from the lake and were rushing across the sky in front of the hotel.

It was...*magnificent.*

'My god! You couldn't have asked for a better advertisement. I hope to goodness someone caught it on camera. I'll bet that blighter Herb did, since I gave his camera back to him not an hour ago,' Oliver laughed.

But Amelia shivered, thinking the flamingos' flight looked more like a desperate escape than a magnificent advertisement.

'Are you alright?' Oliver asked.

'Just someone walking over my grave, I guess,' she replied, still watching the stunning sight.

'In all my years on this island, that is the first time I have seen them do that.'

'Is it an omen?' she asked. 'And if so, can we both please agree that it is a good one rather than a bad one? Especially after my mother's dramatic warning this afternoon.'

'We will most definitely make that assumption, my dear, for what could possibly go wrong now we have all the players held captive on our island? All we have to do is keep them alive until Saturday. Surely that can't be beyond the wit of man, or indeed woman?' Amelia flinched. He was poking fun at her fear for Daisy, laughing at the ease with which Maud had drawn her into an imagined drama.

Amelia squinted her eyes as she looked up into Oliver's face, once again ready to threaten permanent removal of his bridge privileges, when Sawubona and Tantriana glided into the room.

'Felicitations on this blessed evening,' the guru said, pausing just inside the doorway, raising his palms together as if in prayer and bowing deeply, before continuing his glide across the room. Amelia thought he was laying the guru persona on a bit thick, particularly when only she and Oliver were present to witness it. They weren't the ones he was supposed to be impressing, were they?

Oblivious to her silent censure, Sawubona took a seat at the head of the table, the place where Oliver normally sat. Oliver scowled. Amelia grinned, deciding this was punishment enough.

'I'm late with the gong,' Oliver muttered, racing out of the room. Amelia watched Sawubona nod to Tantriana who lifted the lid off the tureen and served the guru with a brim-high serving of gazpacho before taking her seat at his right hand. They tucked into dinner, not bothering to wait for the other guests to arrive.

'As God is my witness, I'll never be hungry again,' Amelia quoted watching the pair gobble down their soup. As a child, the daughter of a playwright and lover of words, Amelia had buried her loneliness and fear by immersing herself in movies, learning every word of dialogue from all the classics.

'*Gone with the Wind,*' Sawubona muttered, slopping up another mouthful of soup.

The gong sounded at ten past eight instead of eight on the dot as promised. It was another ten minutes before Price arrived, quickly followed by Leo and then Wendy. Daisy made a grand entrance, half an hour late, at precisely 8.30 pm. She had pulled out all the stops, dressed in a scarlet evening gown and red-soled Louboutin stilettos. Maud was at least five minutes behind Daisy, and as he had warned might be possible, Amelia's Robinson Crusoe, David, did not turn up at all.

As Sawubona had seated himself at the head of the table, Amelia had no choice but to allow her other guests to pick their own seats too. Truth be told, she resented the time she and Oliver had wasted pre-planning a seating arrangement, though she *was* relieved when Leo took his seat beside her at the foot of the table. She was less thrilled when drab old Wendy Gale sat opposite him on Amelia's other side. But then again, beggars could most definitely not be choosers, and drab though she may be, Wendy was nowhere near the bottom of Amelia's list of preferred dinner companions.

Dinner was more than forty minutes late by the time her guests were finally settled, having helped themselves to soup from the silver tureens. Right at that moment, Herb bustled in, grinning from ear to ear and waving his camera over his head, while simultaneously doing a jubilant little jig. It was quite a horrific sight if you thought about it. Added to which, he had still not changed out of his awful safari outfit, nor did he even bother to apologise for being late to dinner.

Instead, he regaled them with an exciting description of a sight they had all witnessed themselves. 'Did you see those giant bloody birds turn the sky pink like candyfloss? I can sell that shot to *National Geographic* for a flipping mint!' Amelia instantly got over his rudeness, quickly glancing at Oliver who winked. *We have our money shot for our glossy advertising,* the two conspirators silently agreed.

Soon, the soup tureens were drained, and Amelia's guests were tucking-in to heaping plates from the buffet. Well, other than Daisy of course, who was still diligently working her way through a single half-bowl of soup.

Sawubona and Tantriana wolfed down plate after plate from the buffet, acting as if they had never eaten a good home-cooked meal in their lives.

Price and Maud, having seated themselves inconveniently distant and diagonally across from each other, were forced to shout their ever more exaggerated tales of self-aggrandisement and celebrity friendships, drowning out any alternative conversations in the process.

'I met Monica May in Harrods only last week,' Maud bragged, nauseating Amelia, who, glancing around the table, noticed even the grossly spiritual Tantriana and Sawubona raising synchronous eyebrows at *that* little gem.

All the shouting and bragging was irritating, but at least for Amelia—safe at the foot of the table—it diverted Maud's attention from her. She settled into quiet conversation with Leo who, bless his heart, did his utmost to draw Wendy out of her shell. For a first evening entertaining such a mixed bunch, a group who would not necessarily mix in real life, Amelia was quietly satisfied.

It was that quiet satisfaction that inspired Amelia to raise her glass, ready to toast her Uncle Sebastian for his splendid idea of building a healing hotel, and of course darling Oliver for all his help in making it a reality. But just as she lifted her glass, drew in a breath, and opened her mouth to speak, Maud, with impeccable, *deliberate* timing, beat her to it.

'Darlings. I want you, my most intimate of friends, to be the first to know that I, Maud Lavender, will be delighting my many fans worldwide with a spectacular new play. It is so close to completion that I will be presenting it to my many droves of clamouring investors this autumn, ready for a spring opening.'

Her pronouncement was initially met with silence, although Amelia thought she heard Oliver mumble, 'Not without your ghost-writer you won't.'

But Amelia barely noticed Oliver's jibe. She was still absorbing the blow of Maud's obvious attempt to overshadow Amelia's own achievements. *Why do I always get my hopes up? I know she'll never change!*

'Though I will need more *competent* assistance if I am to achieve my deadline,' Maud continued, oblivious to Amelia's hurt while shamelessly contradicting her effusive praise of Wendy earlier that day.

Wendy blanched. Her eyes galloped around the table from person to person.

'Mother!' Amelia hissed, giving Wendy's blush-pink cardiganed elbow a reassuring squeeze.

'It's quite alright,' Wendy said. 'When I took the position, you can be sure I did not expect to find any pleasure in working for your mother. You could say, in that expectation at least, I have not been disappointed.' Maud's mouth hung slackly open as the two women grinned at each other, and for the first time, Amelia saw the other woman's spirit beneath the kicked puppy façade.

'When you told me you were leaving, I almost bolted,' Wendy added with a rueful smile. 'But by then my situation had worsened. The...*attacks*...well, they had escalated, so I had little choice but to take the position, even in light of your warnings and my own reservations.'

Wendy's neck and jaw were tense as she spoke, and though Amelia was certain her mother could produce that look on the face of a saint, she'd seen the same look *before* Maud had ever got her claws into Wendy. In fact, thinking about it with a clear head for the first time, that exact same terrified look had crossed Wendy's face in the driveway when they first arrived at the hotel.

'What happened to you?' Amelia whispered. For a moment, she wasn't sure the other woman would answer her, but after a few frozen seconds, Wendy drew in a sharp breath through her nose, then she puffed it out in three short bursts.

'It's funny Maud should mention Harrods, for that was where my ordeal began one day almost eighteen months ago, not long before Christmas,' she began. 'I was there shopping in the Food Hall for my employer, trying to emancipate a single jar of black truffle puree from a tower piled high to resemble a Christmas tree.

'I felt like a child playing Jenga. I was about to give up when a man in a navy striped suit—he looked like a stockbroker—came to stand next to me,' she said, then corrected herself, 'No, he was shinier than a stockbroker...he looked like *a model* dressed up as a stockbroker. He was tall; so tall that he managed to take a jar from the top of the heap.

'He was shopping for quail eggs and asked if I knew where he might find some. I did not, and for some reason I also told him I had never tasted one. He immediately jumped on that fact. "I must remedy that," he said. And as he seemed harmless enough, when he invited me out for dinner, I jumped at the chance. Who wouldn't when invited by a man who looked like he should be on the cover of *Vogue* and dined on quail eggs?'

'Why are we all so entranced by a dreary story from the hired help? Is my news not sufficiently riveting?' Maud interrupted.

'Ignore your *ex*-employer, dear Wendy, and tell your *new* employer the rest of the story.' Amelia surprised even herself by not-so-subtly offering the fragile woman a much-needed life raft.

'Um...thank you?' Wendy said, before swallowing over an apparent lump in her throat and launching back into her story. 'Well...we went on a couple of dates. He talked incessantly about himself: how successful he was, what clubs he belonged to, the people in high places he not just knew but had some sort of hold over. I was disappointed, because a bully and a braggart are not my idea of the ideal man,' Wendy explained, unconsciously glancing across at Price the exact moment she said the word 'braggart.' A deep flush rose on his cheeks before he scraped back his chair, struggled to his feet, and waddled across to the decanters before pouring himself a large measure of scotch.

'I'd appreciate a top-up myself if we are to be subjected to this sad little story,' Maud called to him, holding out her glass for a refill.

'And...?' Amelia prompted.

'When I explained, quite gently I can assure you, that I didn't believe we were a good fit, he flew off the handle, called me a plain little tease.' She paled and seemed to shrink in her chair as she recalled the incident. 'He stormed off and I thought that would be that. An unpleasant end, but still a relief.'

'But that wasn't that, was it?' Amelia asked.

'No...' Wendy said, shaking her head wearily from side to side. 'It was just the beginning of a nightmare that included a burglary, some very specific and horrific threats, a whole raft of nasty rumours and accusations, all of which culminated in a fire in my lodgings...'

Amelia gasped, just as Leo barked, 'What an absolute bastard!'

'I was so terribly affected that, as you can see, my hair,' she reached a hand up to touch it, 'turned completely white.' Amelia winced. How had the poor woman coped?

'Which is why I was so relieved to be offered a live-in position by your mother.'

It finally makes sense! As horrible as being under Maud's control could be, it would have been nothing when compared to the terror Wendy had experienced.

'It's strange—' Wendy said, but whatever she planned to say was interrupted by Maud.

'What! You brought that...that *baggage* under my roof? What if this devil came looking for you again? Did you ever think of *me*?'

'Mother!'

But the moment was lost. Wendy had ducked her head and had focussed her attention on the food in front of her. Amelia opened her mouth to inquire, but decided it was not the time to push her further. As it was, she looked so fragile that one more question might tip her over the edge. Amelia already had enough on her plate without tears at the table.

The remainder of the meal passed relatively smoothly if you didn't count Daisy alternately fidgeting with her napkin and restlessly popping her knuckles, Price and Maud guzzling down an entire decanter of her best scotch, and Sawubona hoovering up every morsel of food like a ravenous dog at a summer picnic.

It was around 10 pm when, noticing the guests had finished their desserts, Amelia rose to her feet and said, 'If everyone has finished, shall we take coffee in the drawing room?' She didn't wait for a response. Instead, she headed toward the sliding door separating the dining room from the drawing room. She paused before she reached the door to allow her guests to precede her, which they did, filing past her into the lounge. She couldn't help noticing that Wendy still looked pale. On impulse, she reached out to take her by the elbow. 'You're quite safe here, you know,' she told the startled woman. 'Oh, and the job offer was quite genuine if you can face employment with Maud Lavender's daughter.'

'You are probably right, I'm sure I am quite safe. And thank you, Amelia. I'll certainly consider it,' Wendy said as the tide of people carried her through the doorway into the drawing room.

Maud and Price headed directly for the nearest decanter, chatting loudly enough that Amelia could feel the beginnings of a throbbing headache at her temples. So, she was infinitely relieved when they wandered outside onto the veranda, taking their seats at one of the pretty wrought iron tables that overlooked the gardens. *They're as thick as thieves tonight,* Amelia thought. *No doubt they are outside right now, complaining about the accommodations and planning some mischief that I will be unable to prevent.* The very thought of those two vipers out of sight and unsupervised had her right eyelid twitching and her counting the golden rings on the curtain pole above the window.

'Anyone for a rubber of bridge?' Oliver asked, breaking into her thoughts. He gestured toward the table he had set up hours before, determined to unleash his preternatural skills on some unsuspecting opponents.

'You play bridge?' Sawubona asked, his laughing brown eyes alight with excitement. 'Sebastian taught me this game the first time we met. He was travelling through India when he heard about my ashram and...' A slightly panicked look swept across the guru's face, as if he had shared too much. His eyes were no longer laughing when he continued, 'Yes, I would like to play.'

'I'm sure Lia will be playing,' Leo said, seating himself at the table. 'And I will make up the fourth, though I am as much an amateur today as I was the first time dear old Uncle Seb set up this very table in the old house over the way.'

'It's settled then,' Oliver said, pouring out coffee for himself and Amelia and seating himself beside Leo, not opposite. Oliver was competitive and was not about to fall on his sword by pairing himself with bumbling old Leo, the self-proclaimed amateur.

Amelia was ashamed to admit to swerving deeply around Leo to plant herself directly opposite Oliver, leaving Sawubona to pair up with the man she had loved, but whom any sane person would not choose to partner in the game Sebastian Ferver had called *'the game of a lifetime.'*

As they settled, Herb approached the coffee table with a decanter of scotch, ready to pour some into his coffee. 'Anyone else for a nip?' he asked, waving the decanter around like an old-timey mining lamp in a dark cavern. He wandered over to the two sofas close to the dormant fireplace decorated in a mixture of flamingo feathers and wildflowers.

Daisy held out her cup and Herb poured her a shot. Wendy and Tantriana, who were sitting on the second sofa, shook their heads. *He'll charm out all their secrets even without the liquor to loosen their tongues,* Amelia thought. *And then I'll be blamed, and the hotel will be ruined,* Amelia's Inner-Maud told her. She noticed the tell-tale tremor, her hands shaking, as she picked up her cards. *Don't be a goose. It will be their fault if they trust a man who has ruined more promising careers than I've ruined hot dinners,* she thought, shaking off her worry and focusing on her hand.

She and Oliver had lost…to Leo. It was a scandal. Sawubona was a card shark or a grifter or perhaps he had a direct line to some spiritual entity.

'Never beaten Oliver before,' Leo chortled, pounding Sawubona on the back as he left the table to get them all more coffee. Amelia sat frozen in place, facing a slack-jawed Oliver.

'What just happened?' he asked, incredulous, and Amelia burst into gales of laughter. He was in shock.

'It's just one game, darling,' she reassured him. 'They have to beat us again to win the rubber.'

Half an hour later, Amelia's focus was divided between bridge and the rapid deterioration of Daisy's condition. Something was clearly wrong with her. If she didn't know for a fact that Daisy only had one glass of wine with dinner and a small shot of scotch in her coffee, Amelia would have sworn Hollywood's Princess was drunk out of her mind. She started slurring her words about thirty minutes before and was now curled with her feet underneath her, her head leaned against the arm of the sofa. *How is she so drunk? Is she drinking on medication? Is she on drugs?*

'Are you alright, Daisy?' Amelia called.

'Yes, of course, darling. Though I *am* feeling a little sleepy,' she slurred. '*In faaaact,* I think it's time I headed upstairs to Bedfordshire.'

'I can see you up,' Herb offered, jumping to his feet and taking hold of Daisy's hand, ready to pull her to hers.

Amelia thought Daisy might have shivered in revulsion at the clammy fingers grasping her own. The poor girl tried to shake him off, saying, 'Oh no, don't go to any trouble for me.'

'No trouble at all, little darlin'. Good old Herb's dead on his feet too. But there's no sleep for the wicked, at least not until all this evening's juicy gossip is recorded for posterity,' he said, tapping the front pocket of his dreadful khaki shirt, where his paparazzi pad and pen were secreted.

Daisy twisted her neck, hazy eyes sluggishly searching the room for Price, but the man was still outside, gossiping with Maud. So, outmanoeuvred, she rose unsteadily to her feet, and with Herb still not releasing her hand, she nodded and waved her goodnights to Tantriana and Wendy. Herb guided her towards the door, though even with his support, she could barely stand on her designer stilettos.

She should be okay now, Amelia thought, turning her attention back to the game. *She'll sleep soundly and wake up as good as new.*

'Seb never did tell me what moved him to visit your ashram. Care to share, old boy?' Oliver asked, speaking to the guru who was bowing his head, possibly to hide his grin which was so big it looked in danger of splitting his face in two.

'One day I will tell you that story, but for now, my beloved and I must salute the moon and prepare for bed, for we rise with the sun to prepare for tomorrow's puja.'

At his words, Tantriana rose from her seat on the sofa next to Wendy and glided across to him.

'I'm heading up to bed now too. I'll walk up with you,' Wendy said, moving to stand.

'First time I've got anything right in years,' Leo mused, shaking his head and smiling down at the card table.

'You didn't get anything right, old chap. Your new hero Sawubona did.'

'Oh, but I did, my dear boy. I partnered with a master!' Leo chortled, heading to the door, turning only to salute them goodnight before continuing into the hallway and upstairs to bed.

Which left Maud and Price outside and Amelia and Oliver in the drawing room.

'Shall we tidy up the dinner dishes?' Amelia suggested.

'Of course. Only slovens leave dishes to fester overnight.' Oliver smiled. 'And after that, if I know my girl, she'll want to run through tomorrow's itinerary.'

The two of them made light work of the clearing and washing up and were in the office by the time Maud and Price made their way indoors and headed upstairs.

'Almost midnight,' Oliver commented. 'They'd better hurry before one of them turns into a pumpkin at the stroke of twelve.'

Amelia stifled her laugh, not wanting to encourage him. 'I'm heading down to the beach for a swim,' she said. 'Will you come?'

'No, I'm going to finish off here and then I'm heading to bed. It's been a long and tiresome day.'

Amelia popped upstairs to change. On her way to her room, she caught a flash of red out of the corner of her eye. She turned her head just in time to see it disappearing down the back stairs. *Was that Daisy? Wasn't she drunk off her feet an hour ago?* Amelia wondered, before continuing to her room.

Wearing her swimsuit, she descended the stairs, through the jasmine scented gardens, past the pool—she wasn't much of a pool person—and headed for the sloping lawns that descended to the beach.

She was still pondering Daisy's strange behaviour, but then her attention was diverted when she spotted two figures at the far end of the beach, close to the rocks, shrouded in darkness. One looked like David, who hadn't bothered to come up for dinner but seemed perfectly happy to interrupt his tinkering on the yacht for a seaside assignation with a stranger. *Yes, it's definitely him,* she thought, hurrying down the slope, calling out his name as she went. *I'd know that captain's hat anywhere.*

They hadn't heard her yet, but as she hurried closer, could just about make out the second figure. Amelia wasn't sure if it was a man or woman under all the baggy clothing. At a guess they were wearing one of those ponchos for sailing in bad weather, not that Amelia's stomach would countenance such an idea. Or perhaps it was an artist's smock, though both seemed a little odd on a Mediterranean summer evening.

Amelia stopped short. If they hadn't noticed her, why was thundering down the slope, calling David's name, drawing attention to herself? It had been a long day, and she was in the mood for solitude, not company. *But it would be rude to ignore them completely*, she thought.

She stood for a moment, undecided, before raising her hand in a casual wave, and heading, this time more sedately, toward the water.

Neither of the figures even noticed her quandary. They were too busy gesticulating; maybe even arguing. *Maybe I will have to go over in case things escalate*, she thought. But before she was close enough to overhear their words, the stranger clapped David on the shoulder, tapped his temple with his index finger a couple of times in an odd kind of quirky salute, and both stalked away in different directions; David towards the cliff path that led to the jetty, and the stranger along the path that led from the beach towards La Colina Alta where it split in two—one branch leading to the artists' community and the other back to the hotel.

Deep in thought, Amelia tried to push away the day as the serene water lapped at the shore and she waded into its moonlit depths. The beach was wonderfully clean after Pau and David cleared away the seaweed, and as she waded into the water, the sea felt cool and refreshing against her skin. She swam for more than half an hour, keeping within the golden glow of the dual lights from the lighthouse and the hotel. The sea embraced her gently as she alternately swam and floated just far enough from shore to be completely alone, just for a little while. After her bathe she wandered, relaxed and happy, back to the hotel.

As she passed across the pool patio, other than a dim light glowing through her office window, all the bungalows and bedrooms were shrouded in darkness. *Oliver is still working*, she thought, changing course as she entered the French doors and made a beeline for her office. Poking her head around the door, she found Oliver sitting at her desk, staring intently at tomorrow's schedule. She cleared her throat softly so as not to startle him, and said, 'I'm off up to bed. I'll be down at seven to lay out the breakfast. Thanks for all your help today,' then turned away without waiting for a response.

'I'm coming!' he called after her and was soon at her side. They walked upstairs together, then parted on the landing, with Amelia air kissing Oliver on both cheeks, much to his disgruntlement.

Chessie and Tulip were already in her room when she entered, sprawled across her bed, legs stretched to the maximum so there was only a corner of spare space for her.

'You'd better move before I'm out of the shower or you'll be relegated to the parlour,' she told them as she headed to the bathroom. Tulip rolled onto her back and wriggled for a tummy scratch. They wouldn't be moving. And they wouldn't be sleeping in the parlour either.

It felt she'd only been asleep for a matter of seconds when she was woken by the bell at reception. She prised open one eye to peer at the clock on the nightstand; it was after 1.30 am. *Less than a half hour's sleep...* she realised as she staggered half-blind to her bedroom door.

Opening it a chink, she could see Oliver heading down the stairs. Herb was at their foot, leaning over the reception desk, riffling through some papers.

'Get your grubby fingers off my stuff!' Oliver blasted him as he made it to the bottom step. 'Or you'll lose a couple!'

Amelia grinned. *Oliver won't take any nonsense from Herb*, she thought as she shuffled back across the room, climbed back into bed, and snuggled up with her dogs.

She was woken again at two, this time by Tantriana and Sawubona, who had apparently completed their salute to the moon and were now practising a different kind of activity. 'Bloody hell, I hope to goodness they're quick,' Amelia whispered to Chessie.

She didn't get her wish.

CHAPTER SIX

If the alarm clock hadn't insisted it was 7 am, or the birds had been less adamant in announcing the dawn, Amelia could have slept another seven hours straight. A night of fitful half-sleep plagued by Maud-induced nightmares, interspersed with Sawubona and Tantriana's noisy attempts at wrecking a perfectly delightful brand-new wrought iron bed in the adjacent suite, had left her feeling both jetlagged and jaded. On top of that, a rainstorm roused her from bed at 2.30 am. She'd got up to close the windows to shut out the rain, which would no doubt leave a layer of red Saharan dust over everything.

Nevertheless, she dutifully dragged herself into the bathroom for her morning ablutions, then staggered downstairs to help Oliver prepare breakfast.

In the dining room she found him, long-handled dustpan and brush in hand, sweeping clumps of dried seaweed out from beneath the dining table. She would have asked him how he had managed to transport so much of the sea indoors, but instead, she noticed a gauze bandage secured with sticking plaster wrapped around his hand. Amelia had personal childhood experience of Oliver's perfectionistic bandaging, but never, not in her entire time of knowing him, had she seen him wounded, not even a shaving cut. Oliver was not a clumsy man; he was an extraordinarily capable, no-nonsense, military man.

'What have you done?' she gasped, rushing over to him and snatching the brush and pan out of his hands, leaving him both emptyhanded and wincing.

'I was minding my own business, cleaning up half a dozen disgusting cigarette butts from one of those new terracotta planters outside the front entrance, when I was ambushed by a broken piece of glass that had somehow secreted itself there. Both butts and glass shards were *not* there before our esteemed guests arrived.'

Amelia winced. Oliver did not approve of smoking and had painstakingly affixed little brass plaques all around the hotel, warning people that smoking was prohibited. Which, come to think of it, probably accounted for the clandestine butts being disposed of in the planter.

Amelia had seen Price smoking the odd cigar the previous day, and of course, Leo hadn't been able to resist joining him when he'd brandished a box of Fuentes that evening. To be fair, even Sawubona had looked tempted by the Fuentes, before taking a comically slow blink, no doubt reminding himself that gurus were above such mortal temptations. So, plenty of cigar smokers, but she had only seen one person with a cigarette in hand, and that was Herb.

Which reminded her. 'Did you get Herb sorted with whatever his after-midnight complaint was?'

'Yes... He said there was no bulb in the porch light at his bungalow. Funny thing is, I swear I checked all the porch lights earlier in the week. I wonder if one of our guests is a kleptomaniac with a penchant for lightbulbs? I wouldn't put it past any of them,' he mused, shaking his head, brow furrowed. 'Anyway, I gave him a replacement and he never returned, from which I gather the problem was resolved.'

'And after injuring yourself, instead of waking me and asking for help, you butchered yourself with single-handed first aid, proceeded with the juicing of forty oranges, and have now transformed yourself into a one-man clean-up crew?' Amelia asked, while sweeping the last of the dried seaweed into the pan from under the table. It was between Daisy and Herb's place settings from the night before. Then she swept herself, pan in hand, through the swing doors into the adjoining kitchen.

'You're welcome!' Oliver called after her. She was tired and cross even though it wasn't yet seven-thirty in the morning, so although she could hear him perfectly well, Amelia ignored her wounded friend, preferring to slam slices of bread into her industrial-sized toaster and carelessly tip homemade muesli into enormous serving dishes.

No more than ten minutes later, the first of her guests, a surprisingly chirpy looking Tantriana, practically skipped into the room, followed immediately by an equally sprightly Sawubona. Tantriana glowed, and Sawubona looked positively invigorated. Their aliveness couldn't have been more contrary to how Amelia felt, but hey-ho, in two days she would be past the finish line and could sleep for a month if she wanted.

Her other guests sloped into the room a lot less perkily over the next fifteen minutes. As they sipped their coffee and helped themselves to breakfast, Amelia's eyes kept drifting to the empty place setting. It was rather rude of David not to come up to the hotel to chat with her guests. And a little odd, considering one of them was a movie star.

'I've got things handled here,' she said, noticing that Oliver had finished his breakfast. 'Could you pop down to David's bungalow and check on him for me? It's not like him to miss two free meals in a row.'

'On it,' Oliver said, rising to his feet and heading towards the door. 'I'll check all the lightbulbs down at the bungalows while I'm at it,' he added with a wink.

As he strolled out of the room, Amelia turned back to face her guests, ready to explain the itinerary she and Oliver had finalised the night before. 'This morning, at 10 am, we will be taking a gentle hike across to the artists' community, where Barron Lancaster, who as you will no doubt know is a world-renowned impressionist artist, has agreed to give us a tour, including a much-coveted look at his most recent flamingo pieces. When we return—certainly by noon—our gorgeous guru will be leading a cleansing Puja, followed by a lunch of homemade traditional Mallorcan Tumbet out on the pool terrace.

'For those of you who prefer to relax this morning, rather than joining us on our walk, feel free to enjoy the beach and the pool area, as well as the well-stocked library. I'll set you up with provisions in case we take longer than anticipated on our tour.'

'I'm up for a walk,' Leo said.

'Can't think of anything I'd less like to do,' Maud practically snarled. 'The air here is depressingly devoid, especially for those of us who are accustomed to good, strong London air.'

Oliver's Cheshire Cat grin appeared in the doorway. He headed to the coffee pot on the buffet, helped himself to a cup, then approached the table.

'David's bed's not been slept in. Must have spent the night tinkering on the *Titanic*,' Oliver whispered to Amelia. But not quietly enough.

'Titanic?' Price asked, frowning.

'Ignore Oliver. He's just grouchy from his injury,' Amelia said with a grin. 'Dear sweet Oliver likes to tease David about his yacht's sad maiden voyage.'

'You mean there is a means of escape from this island that no one told us about?' Price bellowed.

'Sadly, no,' Amelia reassured him, holding her hands up palms out trying to pacify Price, whose face had turned a worrying shade of red. 'David's been marooned here longer than you have. Even our resident genius Pau can't believe how long the repairs to his yacht are taking. I fear the poor thing might be dead.'

'Come now, Lia, don't be a pessimistic pelican. Jordi is hand-delivering a vital part when he gets back from Mallorca on Saturday. After that it is blue skies and open seas for our Robinson Crusoe,' Oliver chided.

Her guests, most of whom had contributed to the emptying of her drinks cabinet the evening before, had been quiet through breakfast, but were still quieter as they listened to Oliver and Amelia's exchange.

Amelia was pleased to see Daisy, although subdued, was none the worse-for-wear after being escorted to bed. Though she should have guessed as much after seeing her sneaking down the back stairs at midnight. She was going to have to find out what the sneaking around was for; they weren't kids with a curfew anymore, so she really couldn't see any reason for it.

She wondered, not for the first time, if Daisy was on drugs and that was what had her creeping around like a ghoul in the dark; and it might explain her wooziness after her Irish Coffee the evening before.

One thing was certain: Daisy had problems that belied the ecstatic joy-filled, full-page spreads, and the ingenious but ultra-feminine action heroine roles she played in the movies. In fact, Amelia wondered if Daisy had been authentically happy at any time since the kidnapping.

A kidnapping that had never really been solved. Daisy had been snatched, was missing for weeks, and when she was eventually found, a single kidnapper, Paul Vincent, had been apprehended. The consensus was that he couldn't have worked alone, but he said he did. Amelia could not fathom how he had managed to bundle that terrified child into the back of a van and speed off, without at the very least having a getaway driver. And how had this Paul Vincent been planning to collect the ransom while at the same time guarding Daisy?

And that wasn't the only mystery. Why for example, had the newly returned Daisy, a traumatised child, been immediately sent to live with her father in America? Why not her mother? And speaking of Violet Forrester, why did she disappear into thin air the very same day Daisy was found? There were rumours about Daisy's mother; that she'd got involved with a bad crowd; that she was having an affair with a co-star, and that somehow the affair had something to do with the kidnapping. Amelia didn't know what was true and what was gossip. She only knew that all their lives had been irrevocably altered by Daisy's ordeal.

She pushed the kidnapping from her mind. She had other imminent worries.

Images of David drowned, floating face down in the water of the harbour, or crushed by a fallen mast, flashed through Amelia's mind. It just didn't make sense—after all the preparation and the millions of unasked-for opinions from David on the minutiae of her party planning, why on earth would he closet himself away in his boat? That had her worried. Even that weird tension with her guests outside the hotel the day before didn't explain his absence.

Stop catastrophising! He's probably cooking himself up some breakfast before cracking on with his to-do list.

She had to go and check on him though. If she didn't, she knew her head would explode with worry and poor injured Oliver would be left to clean up the bloody detritus.

After breakfast was over and her guests had dispersed to their rooms or the beach, Amelia departed for the harbour to placate her internal Pessimistic Pelican. At least she made it to the car before, once again, she was ambushed by Miserable Maud, who intercepted her as she crossed the courtyard.

'I will keep you company on your journey,' she said. Amelia glanced at her mother whose face was pinched in disgust as she wiped red dust from the car door handle before swinging it open and wiping down the white leather seat. Last night, that unusual summer rainstorm had combined with the Sahara dust plume drifting overhead to coat her car and everything else with a thick layer of dust.

Amelia, not expecting rain, hadn't bothered to draw the Caddy into the garage last night—not that it mattered terribly. The Mediterranean sun had already dried everything out, leaving only a little harmless red dust in its wake. Amelia had grown accustomed to the red rain here on El Pedrusco, but Maud's expression indicated she would never get used to it, which didn't hurt Amelia's feelings one bit.

'You don't even know where I'm going. Aren't you worried I'll feed you to the sharks?'

'Not one bit,' Maud said. 'There are no sharks who are wont to feast on me, not in the Mediterranean.'

'I could push you off the cliff,' Amelia suggested, surprising herself with her temerity.

'You could,' Maud agreed. 'But that would hardly be good for business, would it?' She climbed into the passenger seat.

Amelia only had thirty minutes before she was due to meet with her guests in reception; she didn't have the time to argue. So, she said nothing, threw the car into drive, and sped off down Highway One.

As they passed the lighthouse, Amelia spotted Pau standing on the gallery deck, holding a steaming cup of coffee, and gazing across La Colina towards the hotel. He waved when he spotted her, and she blew him a kiss, grateful for a distraction from Maud's droning diatribe about 'the unbearable plebs' she was forced to sit beside on the flight from Heathrow.

At last, they reached the marina. It was empty other than David's yacht moored at the small jetty.

'You wait here while I check on David,' Amelia instructed, opening the car door and heading for the yacht. Maud *harumphed*, though she did remain seated.

David wasn't on deck when she reached the yacht. *He must be below,* she thought as she called out, 'Yoo-hoo,' and climbed aboard without invitation. She waited a beat for a response, but hearing none, she slipped off her shoes. The deck was covered by a layer of dust, just as her Caddy had been. She'd be cleaning from now until the moment the rest of the party guests arrived on Saturday, no doubt.

'Cooee. David, are you here?' she called as she padded across to the cabin hatch and knocked firmly. Nothing.

Amelia's stomach-dwelling boulder rocked inside her, pounded on a sea of dread. *'This isn't right,'* she muttered, grabbing the handle.

The day was already beyond warm, and as she slid open the hatch the metallic smell of blood, coupled with a nauseating fruity aroma, hit her nostrils and she gagged. Bile rushed up from her stomach into her throat, and she reared back, away from the hatch. She must have made a sound, probably a horrified shriek, because moments later Maud was up the ladder and standing beside her on the boat.

'What's that ghastly smell?' she asked, not hesitating for one second to remove her heels before clip-clopping straight past Amelia and down the ladder, disappearing below deck.

But Amelia *was* hesitating. She was reliving the teenage memory of the day she had found the body of an elderly stagehand named Malcolm, who had fallen from the rigging above the stage after one of Maud's plays. Everyone had assumed at the time that he had climbed up there after the last performance of a not particularly successful run, and jumped. Everyone but Amelia that was. And she had quickly proved otherwise...

But now wasn't the time to think about poor Malcolm's murder. Amelia was frozen to the spot by the olfactory memory of a body left undiscovered, centre stage, for three long days. *Eight hours here in the damp heat of the Balearics might do the same amount of damage as three full days in London in late autumn.* She retched at the thought, but quickly recovered herself.

'Mother!' Amelia called, hurrying down the ladder, hoping to prevent the inevitable. But before she made it to the bottom rung, Maud let out a wail the likes of which Amelia hadn't heard for fifteen years.

Still on the ladder, she spun around to face a horrifying scene. There, lying precariously close to a dead body—David's dead body—was Maud. As Amelia's feet hit the floor, Maud opened her eyes and began to wail.

Amelia reached out her arms, muttering soothing platitudes, 'It's okay. I'm here. I'm coming to get you.' As she trod carefully around the pool of blood, every muscle in her body was screaming at her to turn and run, but her mother was lying on the floor beside a corpse, which meant her long-ingrained protective instinct had kicked into action.

Having negotiated her way around David's body, she tried to heave Maud to her feet, but she was limp, a dead weight. Amelia hiccupped out a sob, then grabbed hold of one of her mother's arms and dragged her along on her back across the floor before lugging Maud's quivering body up into a seat.

'I–is he...*dead?*' her mother stuttered, her normally strident voice breaking as she forced out the words. Amelia needed to calm her down, so she squeezed her shoulder and turned her face away from David. What she did not do was respond to Maud's question.

A question which had an obvious answer if you looked at David's faceless corpse. Shock had frozen her tongue to the roof of her mouth and welded her jaw tightly shut.

Amelia closed her eyes to the scene, dragging in deep breaths as Maud sat panting like Tulip after a fruitless rabbit chase up the side of the mountain. *In for the count of four, out for the count of six.* This was the rhythm Amelia had learned as a child to calm her mother's frequent bouts of hysteria, and it was perhaps the origin of Amelia's own love of counting. 'In for four, out for six,' she whispered, crouching down to take Maud's hands. 'In for four, out for six,' she repeated over and over until they had both stopped shaking and their breathing was less ragged.

You need to open your eyes. It took some doing; they felt glued shut. But she did open them and scanned the room, really taking in the full extent of the mess for the first time.

She spotted a small fridge in the galley. She hurried over and snatched open the door. She was looking for bottled water for Maud, but instead of water, she found the fridge stuffed to the gunnels with cash. American dollars to be precise. The bills were in three large stacks, each one made up of half-inch-thick bundles. She reached in and took hold of one of the bundles, saw Benjamin Franklin's face staring up at her. Something in the back caught her eye. *Are those passports?*

Again she reached into the fridge and pulled them out. Two were red and one was blue-black. British passports...three of them, the variety of colours indicating that they were issued in different eras.

Behind her, Maud groaned. So, Amelia shoved the passports and a single bundle of cash into the back pocket of her shorts and went back to scanning the cabin for water. *Bingo!* she thought, when she spotted a six-pack of litre bottles half-hidden on the floor beneath the dining table. She quickly wrenched one out of the plastic wrapper and scuttled back to Maud, who was sitting, eyes closed, grey-faced, mouth hanging half-open and listing to one side.

Amelia touched the bottle to Maud's parted lips and tipped a little into her mouth. Maud swallowed, coughed, and then let out a long moan, before finally shifting to a more upright position.

'Everything is ruined,' Maud half-spoke, half-wailed. 'The police must be called, and they will force you to cancel the opening. *You will lose everything!*' Maud's final words built into a screeching crescendo.

Amelia tilted her head to one side. Was that a smile on Maud's lips? *No!* Even Malignant Maud wouldn't dare to capitalise on a man's death...would she?

'You must come home... I insist! This place will have nothing but terrible memories now,' Maud decided, confirming Amelia's suspicions and consequently rebreaking her oft-broken heart. Anger flooded her veins, creeped up her neck and turned her cheeks a deep shade of red. *How dare she? How dare she be so absolutely bloody horrid!*

And in response to the powerful anger, words emerged from Amelia almost of their own volition. 'I won't be calling the police, dear mother, because I can't. We have no means of communication until the yacht returns.'

This wasn't true. Amelia's emergency radio was sitting safely in her desk drawer at this very moment, but Maud didn't need to know that.

'We must solve it ourselves. The show must go on after all. Isn't that what you told me time and time again when you had writer's block and your own future was at stake? Aren't those the very words you used to make me craft your plays when you were "far too traumatised" to do it yourself?'

Maud didn't respond, though she did tip her head back and place the back of her hand—with characteristic drama—against her forehead. She groaned before listing sideways once again.

Amelia straightened her shoulders and looked around the cabin, trying to focus. She had just announced she was going to solve David's murder, but she was no sleuth. Like the masses, Amelia appreciated a good Agatha Christie mystery movie at Christmas, but now that she was thrown into the middle of one, she felt completely outmatched.

For once, Maud is right. I have to radio the police.

Standing stock still, she scanned the room for clues. There was the money and the passports that were now hidden away in her pocket.

There was a lamp on the floor, two chairs were overturned, an old copy of the *Barco-lona* magazine lay face down and splashed in blood on the floor, a low mahogany filing cabinet was laying on its side with its drawers closed, which meant—according to any mildly competent fictional sleuth—this was not a burglary gone wrong. *After all, the thief hasn't taken the oodles of cash secreted in the fridge, and hasn't every mystery movie ever made shown us quite clearly that, when looking for jewels, or drugs, or cash, one should always search inside the fridge first?* And even though she wasn't a fictional sleuth, let alone a criminal mastermind, it made no sense for any self-respecting robber to burgle a broken-down boat when there was a glamourous new hotel a stone's throw away.

Okay, what else? Amelia asked herself, at last turning her attention to the body. There was no avoiding it. He was lying on his back, one arm stretched out to the side waist high, the other flung over his head. David was wearing the same clothes as the day before.

Peeking out from beneath his bloody collar, Amelia noticed the faint glint of gold. She reached out, carefully pushed back the fabric with the back of her hand and tugged the chain free. Dangling from it was an ornate key. There was an engraving around the oval bow, but as she moved it about, she couldn't clearly see what it read.

She didn't have time to investigate further now, so she jerked hard on the key, once, twice, three times, until the fine chain broke. Maud gasped; Amelia ignored her. Quickly she stuffed the jewellery into her empty back pocket, then stood from her crouch and scanned the cramped compartment, thinking and trying to remember every detail from when she had last seen David from up on her mountain. He'd been sitting up on deck, lounging on his deck chair in the shade of his parasol, papers scattered all around him as he worked, briefcase at his feet. Glancing around the room again, Amelia realised his briefcase was missing. *Another clue!*

She searched the cabin. The engine hatch was open, so she poked her head in there just to be certain it was missing. No briefcase, but the tools David had been using to repair the engine were laid out neatly on his workbench.

Having exhausted herself, and any obvious clues, Amelia pulled the three passports out of her pocket and opened one of the red ones. The passport had another six years to run, it was issued in the name David Ash, and it had a fairly recent photo of the man lying at her feet.

She could hear Maud moving around behind her, so she turned back to the galley as she opened the second red passport. This one was in the name of Dominic Strathclere, and just like the other passport, the photo was recent. Mind racing, Amelia flipped open the last passport. This one was much older and was one of the blue-black ones that had been phased out five or six years earlier. There were two photos in this one. The first was David as a spikey-haired, pre-teen and the second was of him in his twenties. Although dated, the photos were him, but in this passport his name was Corey Wilson.

Amelia read the names again, this time aloud to press them into her memory, 'David Ash, Dominic Strathclere, Corey Wilson.'

She heard a deep intake of breath. She looked up from the passport and saw that, if it was possible, more blood had leached out of Maud's already pallid face.

'What's wrong?'

Maud looked blank for a moment, like a computer that had gone offline, before she recovered herself sufficiently to snap, 'A man is dead, right in front of me. What could possibly be wrong?'

Amelia righted the overturned chair and plonked herself down into it. Her mind was whirring. All that cash. Why would David stay here, working on the opening, when he had more than enough money to buy the parts and make the repairs to his yacht?

David was on her island for a reason, and that reason might just be the motive in his murder.

She tilted her head down to look at the three passports clasped in her hand. They raised two immediate questions. First, what kind of a person would need three passports? Second, why would someone in possession of two fake passports keep them, one even after it had expired.

Her answer to the first question was simple: David was a man with something or many somethings to hide.

As to the second question, Amelia could only guess. Was it possible that David Ash had an attachment to the name Corey Wilson? Had something happened back then, when he was Corey Wilson, that had caused him to invent a new identity? Did he hold fond memories as Corey that he couldn't quite let go of?

For Amelia, if they said anything at all, those passports implied that the motive for this crime lay somewhere not on this island, but in the past of David Ash, Dominic Strathclere or Corey Wilson.

And there was no mistaking that her mother had gasped aloud at one of those names. She'd clammed up straight after, covered her tracks with a nasty jibe, but she'd given herself away. Maud knew something, and come hell or high water, Amelia was going to find out what it was.

'Which name did you recognise, Mother? Was it David Ash? Dominic Strathclere? Or was it Corey Wilson?' she asked, watching Maud's face closely. One small wince, but Amelia couldn't tell if it was Strathclere or Wilson that had her flinching. Either way, Maud had unwittingly confirmed some knowledge of the crime, and so, sadly, became Amelia's very first suspect.

'I don't know what you are talking about,' Maud blustered. 'I've had a terrible shock. Would it be too much to ask for you to cover the body?' she pleaded. Amelia sighed deeply and nodded in a silent agreement.

Two hours later, Amelia and her mother were collapsed into high-backed chairs in the hotel drawing room, Amelia staring at her shoes while her mother knocked back her fifth gin martini.

At the *Titanic*, once her mother had recovered sufficiently to stand, Amelia had helped her off the yacht and across the tarmac to the Cadillac, sending her on an errand to fetch Oliver. With his military training, she felt he might know best how to store the body while they waited for the police. She would have gone herself, but who knew what Maud might do. Besides, she had more searching to do in the time between Maud leaving the marina and Oliver returning with his Land Cruiser and a heavy tarpaulin. That, and she didn't need Maud hovering while she radioed for help with the yacht's radio.

But then, when she looked, there was no radio—not anymore. The murderer had taken something heavy to it, leaving it smashed beyond repair. *What on earth is going on?* Amelia thought desperately. *Calling the police will have to wait until I get back to my office.*

Amelia made the most of her time alone searching through David's belongings again. There were a couple of waterproof plastic storage boxes; one containing an assortment of Sellotape, scissors, pencils, elastic bands, sticky-note pads, and a couple of magazines. It was as if someone had tipped the contents of the kitchen drawer into it. The other bag was filled with more tools, not dissimilar to the ones she had seen laid out immaculately by the open engine compartment day after day over David's entire stay on the island.

Oliver had arrived, his Land Cruiser puttering down the slope into the marina. As he climbed out of the vehicle, face pale and pinched, Amelia's resolve dwindled, and she morphed back into that same timid girl she had been a year earlier.

Oliver's first words, upon seeing her red-eyed look of utter hopelessness, were, 'Don't you even consider crawling back into your shell and dutifully skulking back off to London in that merciless tyrant's wake! If you lose everything, well, so be it! But don't you bloody dare go down without a fight.' And with that he had marched up the gangplank and onto the *Titanic*.

'Surely,' he called over his shoulder, 'with such a teensy little pool of suspects, and...' He turned his wrist to glance at his watch. '...a full thirty-four hours before the party, it is not beyond the wit of man—or in this case, *woman*—to figure out who would want to do away with Mr Mushy Peas.

'And when we get back to the hotel—' he lowered his voice to a whisper, even though there was only a mutilated dead man below deck to overhear them '—we can use that radio you have secreted in your desk drawer to call the Guardia Civil to save us.'

Amelia would have mentioned the ship's radio if she'd still been listening. Instead, she patted the pocket on the righthand side of her shorts, feeling the outline of three passports. If she wanted to know who the killer was, she needed to figure out who the victim was, and these passports might just be the key.

CHAPTER SEVEN

Amelia was worried. She needed to talk to Oliver immediately, but he was off cleaning up the crime scene.

On her return to the hotel, she had checked her desk drawer, only to find it empty. Well, not empty exactly; there was a notepad and some pens, a calculator, odds and ends...but no radio.

Her heart was pounding in her chest by the time he arrived back with the body at 11 am. He had enlisted Pau's help in transporting it, and a jittery Amelia watched as the two of them struggled to unload it from the Land Cruiser, then half-carry, half-drag the tarp-wrapped corpse across her beautiful foyer into the kitchens. There they deposited it like a bag of groceries into one of the big chest freezers which had, until that moment, been reserved for all her wonderful homegrown produce.

Amelia watched anxiously from the reception area, imagining the recumbent faceless corpse surrounded by frozen asparagus spears and French beans. She shook her head, trying to clear it, and when she was finished, Pau had gone, and Oliver was standing in front of her with a frown marring his noble features.

'My radio is gone,' she whispered.

'The one from your desk drawer?' he asked, his eyebrows disappearing into his hairline.

'Yes, that one,' she replied. 'And the one on David's boat was sabotaged as well... which means we're cut off completely until Saturday.'

'So it would seem. It looks like the scoundrel is heavily invested on keeping the rest of us right where we are. The question is why?'

'And who?' Amelia added.

'Of course,' Oliver agreed, before patting her awkwardly on the shoulder and walking away.

Amelia was left standing alone, feeling as lonely and afraid as she ever had.

She didn't move for five full minutes, not a whisker...and then some inner resilience—what remained of her untapped determination that had driven her forward to this day—kicked in. It came, distressingly, in the guise of Inner-Maud. But it came, and for now that was all that mattered.

Are you going to just stand here while your dream slips between your fingers?

'No,' she whispered, hesitantly.

Then how about you get on with something useful? Like lunch! the voice ordered. *Your thinking is always sharper on a full stomach and what would be the use of solving the crime—and thus saving your hotel—if your guests upped and left before the opening due to malnourishment?*

When she entered the kitchen, she carefully avoided the big chest freezer. Instead, she walked directly to the food preparation area and began preparing the Tumbet. Her mind churned as she sliced aubergines, peeled and sliced potatoes, then began to fry them. *Where do I start?* she wondered.

Do you really think because you wrote a couple of mystery plays you can solve a real murder? Inner-Maud's voice sniped. Amelia tossed two cups of courgettes into the frying pan.

As she worked, she realised she *could* use that experience to help her now. Maud had relied on Amelia to research and plot her stage plays, which meant she really *did* know where to start.

With the characters.

Writing was telling stories, but Amelia had always been fascinated by the *characters*.

In a murder mystery, the main characters were the victim, the sleuth, and the murderer. Sadly, the victim had already been cast, and it seemed—for the second time in her life, if you counted the untimely demise of Malcolm the stagehand—Amelia had been forced by circumstances into the role of sleuth. Which left the murderer, and right then, all the island's residents—temporary and permanent—were potential murderers. They were her limited suspect pool.

Good. She was getting somewhere. Two roles cast and a bunch of actors at a real-life casting call for the part of murderer. In a play, when she was thinking about suspects, she gave some of them the means, some the opportunity, and some the motive. She was careful to make sure only the murderer had all three.

Amelia smiled. There was little she liked more than a well-structured plan, and through her experience in the theatre, she had happened on a simple one to root out a murderer. When she had finished cooking, she would sit down to lunch with her suspects, and while they relaxed on the patio, eating and drinking in the shade of oversized parasols, she would take her first real step to becoming the detective.

In the meantime, she had three other mysteries to consider. First, there was the victim. The choice of victim held potent clues to motive. Before the crime, Amelia had taken David's presence on her island at face value, but now he had been murdered, and after finding all that money and *three* passports in his fridge, she realised that he hadn't happened upon her island by accident. He too had been playing a part, and those three identities suggested that he had spent a lifetime lying. It was her job to expose those lies now.

But perhaps David was a conundrum I should leave for a time when I'm not juggling knives.

Which reminded her of the second mystery: the weapon. As far as Amelia could tell, David's injuries could only have been caused by a gun. But she had already searched the boat from top to bottom without finding one, which meant she either hadn't searched hard enough, or the murderer had taken the gun with them.

And then there was the third mystery: the time of death. If she was going to interrogate her suspects for alibis, she certainly needed to narrow the current nine-hour window.

But how the devil do I do that?

She had seen David on the beach at around midnight, which meant thirty minutes later—it took more than half an hour to walk from the beach to the *Titanic*—he could have been back on his yacht, ready to be murdered. She and Maud hadn't arrived at the crime scene until after 9 am, which left a very large window of opportunity for the murderer.

She sucked in a breath and rolled her shoulders. All this thinking was making her tense.

I know! I'll make a pie, she thought.

You have never successfully baked a pie in your life! Inner-Maud reminded her.

There's a first time for everything, she replied, mentally poking her tongue out.

Amelia sprinkled flour onto the clean, black granite worktop before slapping the dough onto it. Clouds of flour puffed into the air before falling onto the surface, making Rorschach patterns beneath and around her ball of dough. Grabbing a rolling pin, she began to flatten out the crust, rolling it rhythmically backward and forward across the dough, counting out each sweep; *one, and back, two and back...*

The rhythm soothed her laboured mind. She peeled back the dough, sprinkled more flour, and started rolling it again. Her mind settled, her jumbled thoughts became the dough and the flour. Then, her breathing eased, and as she peeled back the dough for a second time, she noticed more Rorschach patterns forming from the dampness of the dough mixing with the powdery flour. The worktop was smeared.

In a flash she remembered the red rain. The way Maud had smeared the layer of dust into the leather as she wiped the car seats. Oliver's footprints on the terrace...

The deck of David's boat was a pure layer of dust. No smears, no footprints, just the flour without the dough.

No one entered or left that yacht after the rainstorm at 2.30 am. Eureka! David must *have been killed between 12.30 am and 2.30 am.* Amelia straightened, growing in stature as she realised that she had made her first true discovery.

Maybe I really can solve this murder and save my inheritance, she thought as she went back to making a pie that had been inspirational but would, no doubt, turn out to be as inedible as every other pie she had ever made.

At Amelia's request, for lunch Oliver had arranged the tables on the pool terrace into one large table. Food and wine had been served, and her guests were consuming both with various levels of enthusiasm.

Amelia, having diligently prepared and served the meal, was lost in thought while her guests ate silently. Everyone knew what had happened. While she was cooking, Maud had apparently recounted the events of that morning. Most likely with relish.

Amelia's thoughts were like the opening credits of *Star Wars:* an open expanse of space with words scrolling upwards; a list of names. *My suspects.* The list was long, but she knew, with her new shorter window for time of death, she had some hope of whittling it down to just a few.

No, she had to find the *one.*

But who are the most likely suspects? Leo? Daisy? That imbecile Price? Wendy of all people? What possible reason could any of them have to kill a man they had only met that day?

Though, she remembered that when they met, there had been shock all around...shock and animosity. But Amelia didn't think she could bear it if the murderer turned out to be one of the people she loved.

Or Maud? She didn't want a murderer for a mother, and mendacious as she was, surely not even Maud would...

No! She dragged her thoughts back to her plan. She would focus on means, motive, opportunity. The greatest of which must be opportunity, for it was true that a motive was irrelevant if they had no opportunity to commit the crime.

She was confident that at least a few of the faces around the table hadn't had any opportunity. In fact, she knew at least one already. *Oliver.*

It was true Oliver had never warmed to David, and he *did* have that nasty cut on his hand in the morning, but he had been working in their office when Amelia returned from her swim. The hotel and bungalows had been dark when they had gone upstairs together, and he had been at the front desk with Herb at 1.30 am. She was certain, being in all those places, he hadn't enough time to get to the marina, murder David, and get back before the rain.

Does that 1.30 am. call put Herb in the clear too? And how did that pesky bulb go missing?

She could cross the energetically noisy Sawubona and Tantriana off the list. Her own disrupted sleep was their alibi. Which left Maud, Price, Daisy, Leo, Wendy, and Herb from the hotel, plus there was Pau at the lighthouse, and the three artists: Beatrice, Barron, and Hank the shadow artist.

She would need to visit Pau and the artists that afternoon. But first...

Heart thrumming in her chest, Amelia raised her eyes from her plate and scanned the table for a murderer. She paused to study each of her guests in turn. She needed to prise alibis out of this motley crew. But how?

'Maud tells us the yacht guy is dead. Murdered,' Price said, interrupting her thoughts. 'How do you plan to contact the po-lice while we're stranded on this blasted rock with no phone?'

'Stranded and in danger of being murdered!' Maud added, her voice shrill with fear. Amelia ignored her. She was used to Maud's fear. It burned hot and bright but died down quickly.

'Unfortunately, there is no way of contacting them, Mr Whitney,' Amelia replied, taking a fortifying sip of wine before continuing. 'For now, we are going to have to do our best to find the culprit ourselves. With a little mutual honesty, diligent investigation, and a peppering of luck, we should have some answers by the time the rest of our guests arrive for the grand opening tomorrow evening. Perhaps it will put your mind at ease to know that the chief of the Guardia Civil and his lovely wife will be one of those arrivals?'

'And how, little lady, do you propose to root out this goddamn groundhog?' Price asked. Amelia ignored the unwanted endearment and focused on the question.

'Well...if you mean how will we unmask our killer, perhaps you would be kind enough to start us off by sharing your whereabouts between midnight and 2.30 am.'

'Are you accusing dear Price of murdering that odious man?' Maud erupted.

'What do you mean *odious*, Mother?'

Maud's face slammed shut, and she shook her head, refusing to answer.

Amelia sighed. 'And for your information, I'm not accusing Price. I'm asking for his alibi. To *exclude* him. You do realise it could have been any one of us that killed David?'

'Killed by some drifter after his money,' Price muttered, before continuing. 'Not sure you'd call reading crappy scripts in bed before turning in at around one an alibi, but...' He shrugged his big shoulders, leaving his sentence unfinished.

'Or it could be the same person who stole my party dress,' Daisy mused, before saying, 'But whoever it was, I know it can't have been Peppy. He was comforting me after I disturbed him with my nightmares. You brought me a glass of water,' she reminded him, glancing around the table. 'And if you remember, Peppy, you stayed for an absolute age, chattering away about nothing in particular...to distract me.'

Amelia strongly suspected that was a lie. Hadn't she glimpsed the red of a gown or nightdress leaving the hotel by the back staircase before her swim? And Price's demeanour didn't exactly scream chatty. Was it possible that Daisy was fabricating an alibi either for Price or for herself?

Now wasn't the time to force the issue—not in front of an audience. She'd find a time to be alone with Daisy and she'd ask her then. For now, both their names would remain on Amelia's suspect list.

'Can't you see that Price has already provided you with your answer? A vagrant broke into his vessel to steal that big pile of money, was discovered by David, and then the burglar killed him in order to get away!' Maud insisted.

'This island isn't exactly brimming with vagrants,' Oliver cut in, stifling a grin.

Amelia stared daggers at Maud. She had appeared genuinely shocked at the murder scene. Now, it seemed, she had been busily taking notes ready to spill the beans to gain favour with a Hollywood agent.

'No, not brimming with them,' Amelia agreed. 'But Maud is right. There *was* an enormous amount of cash on that boat. It could be connected.'

'How much? And where is it now?' Leo asked, leaning forward, elbows on the table.

'I didn't stop to count it, but I wouldn't be surprised if there was $100,000. Happily, it is now locked away in my safe, where it will stay until the Guardia arrive.'

'You know dear, $100,000 would go a long way towards financing my play,' Maud mused.

'That's a great deal of money to leave lying around on a boat,' Price said.

'It was a surprise to us all,' Oliver drawled. 'For didn't he limp into our harbour aboard a wounded yacht, then scrimp and save the pittance Amelia paid him? Why not splash some of that immense stash of cash and pay for the parts he needed outright?'

Blank looks all around.

Amelia wanted to shake someone. All the furtive looks and long pauses in conversation were not getting her anywhere.

'What about you Leo?' Amelia asked.

Leo looked confused, then cornered. Then, he swallowed, his Adam's apple bobbing, before answering. 'Fraid to say, I'm utterly alibi-less, my old duck. Slept like a log, woke at seven, took a shower, then came down to breakfast.' Amelia hoped it was true, but she still sensed her old chum was holding something back. *Is there more to his story of ruin in London?*

She didn't get the chance to probe further because Wendy, who'd been hunched over in her seat, trying not to attract attention for the entire length of the meal, spoke. Her voice was hesitant, but clear.

'You are certain the man you call David is dead?' she asked.

'Oh yes, he's dead as a dodo, my dear,' Oliver replied. 'Does that bring you relief?' Amelia frowned at Oliver. *What an odd thing to ask.*

'Well, sad as it is when anyone dies...it is, as you say, a relief.'

'But why? You barely met the man. Never spoke a single word to him,' Leo asked.

'Oh...yes. That would seem strange, wouldn't it?' Wendy said, then turned to look directly into Amelia's eyes. Hers were a pale powder-blue. *Strange I hadn't noticed that before,* Amelia thought. *But then again, I'm not even certain Wendy has ever looked directly at me before. What has changed?*

'Um...well...you remember the man I described to you last night? My stalker?'

'Yes, of course we all remember.'

'Well, *his* name was Dominic Strathclere. And I could have sworn he was the man you know as David. When he was standing outside the hotel yesterday afternoon, I froze. I had no idea what to do. Had he followed me here? Was I in danger?'

Her voice fell away, though the other voices rose in a barrage of questions, making Wendy sink back into her chair.

Amelia's mind was racing. Wendy had recognised David on sight and said nothing. And she wasn't the only one who had been affected by that scene outside the hotel. Maud had been frozen in place too, and *she* had later recognised one of the names in those two surplus passports, one of which was issued in the name of Wendy's stalker. *Bloody Maud! She knows something, so why isn't she speaking up?*

I need to talk to them all privately. She picked up her knife, felt the weight of it in her hand, then took up the fork to finish her meal, eyes wandering from guest to guest.

Daisy rose jerkily to her feet, reaching one hand out to Price who was sitting beside her. 'I need some time to recover from the shock,' she said, grasping him by the shoulder, then leaning into him and hissing, 'I can't stand it! The way they're all ogling me. It's worse than the paparazzi!' With that, she set off across the patio toward the hotel.

'I'm not ogling, Daisy. I'm as shocked as the rest of you,' Amelia called out to her retreating back.

'Shocked? Perhaps...but you've certainly bounced back sufficiently to conduct this interrogation, haven't you? It is becoming clear that you would arrest even your own mother if it would save this ridiculous enterprise!' Maud accused, her voice a sledgehammer of recrimination. 'So, in the hopes of saving myself from the horrors of a Spanish gaol, I will share my whereabouts, after which you might be kind enough to leave me in peace.'

Maud cleared her throat, raising her voice theatrically. 'I retired a little before midnight, but as you know, I am exceedingly vigorous for my age. So, even after a long day of travel, I found myself unable to sleep.

'Deciding on a moonlight stroll, I took what I thought was the beach path. But after ten minutes or so walking, I found myself nowhere near the beach. I was quite lost. It is so easy to take a wrong turn on an unlit path, don't you think?' she asked Price.

It was a dig, of course. But a fair one. Amelia made a mental note to buy some of those little solar lanterns to light the path.

'I persevered, intrepid in my exploration, and was rewarded an hour later by the welcome sight of a little gaggle of huts nestled into the side of the mountain. It was the artists' village you planned on taking us to this morning.'

Funny how Maud hadn't mentioned these events when she'd turned her nose up at a visit to the artists' community that morning. 'There I was welcomed by a perfectly delightful French artist who later guided me back to the hotel path. I did not check the time when I returned, but I would hazard a guess it was 2 am. I spotted dear Herb leaving reception just before I entered. After that, I slept as well as one can on a lumpy mattress.'

After Daisy's exit and Maud's unnecessarily long-winded explanation, which by no means took her off the suspects list, lunch became an uncomfortable affair. Everyone focused intently on their food, praising the chef and then, one by one, they disappeared back into the hotel.

Eventually, Amelia was left sitting alone at a table strewn with the debris of the meal. She had more questions to ask, but her guests'/suspects' emotions had been stirred up. She would give them some space before speaking to them individually.

She caught sight of Beatrice leaving the Shrine Room. *Probably on her way back to the artists' community after leaving her daily offering. Maybe I'll head over there now to establish their alibis—including my mother's. Besides, the dogs need to stretch their legs and it will give me some space to think.*

CHAPTER EIGHT

Tulip and Chessie were dancing around her feet as she grabbed her old olivewood staff and headed out of the hotel. They'd been cooped up indoors all morning, so the dogs weren't doing the best job at containing their exuberance.

She took the rough path behind the hotel, which meandered through the foothills until it split. The lefthand fork led to the lighthouse and on to the marina. The other path veered sharply to the right, continued for a further two hundred metres where it split again, with one fork leading to the beach and the other heading down a winding slope into the centre of the artists' community.

She breathed more freely the further away she got from her suspects. She had a banging headache after the drama at lunch, so she focused on the abundant wildlife and her dogs rolling in goodness-knew-what as they frolicked in the sunshine.

The boulder in her stomach receded as she walked, though she couldn't shake the feeling she was being watched. As she reached the place where the path split, she glanced over her shoulder for what felt like the hundredth time. *Was that something moving in the brush? No, you're imagining things!*

She refocused. If she went to the lighthouse, she could ask Pau about his movements the night before and find out if he'd heard anything down at the marina. From the deck of his lighthouse, he had a clear view of David's yacht in its mooring.

But with Maud keeping secrets, perhaps she should head straight for the artists' community to see if her alibi held water?

She might have stood there forever if her lolloping hounds had not made the decision for her, chasing a rabbit, real or imagined, along the split in the path that headed for the lighthouse.

A noise came from her left and both dogs came tearing back to her, coming to heel, as more crunching and the odd expletive sounded from a small copse of trees. As she rounded the next bend, she spotted Herb staggering around, binoculars and camera around his neck. He looked startled, as if he'd been caught spying on someone. In one way,

Amelia breathed freer knowing she wasn't being stalked by some sinister force—just a paparazzo with a camera. *He must have been out here for a while,* she thought, noting the pink of his skin and the dampness of his clothing. *Come to think of it, he wasn't at lunch.*

'Everything okay?' Amelia asked as she approached.

'Just takin' in the air,' he replied, moving to her side. 'So, where are you headed? Just out for a walk?'

Why is it, when you're rooting out a murderer, everyone starts acting creepy? Amelia wondered, hurrying back to the path.

'Yes, the dogs need a run to burn off some of this excess energy.'

'Mind if I tag along?' Herb asked, hurrying after her.

Amelia did mind, but years of Maud-related diplomacy prevented her from admitting as much. So, she continued on her way, not bothering with small talk. Herb did not do the same.

'Do you think young Daisy is alright?'

'I hadn't really thought about it,' she replied, lying. 'What makes you ask?'

'Last night, she 'ad maybe two drinks, but she was like a ragdoll when I took her up to her room.'

'Yes, I noticed that. Perhaps she was just tired from the journey?'

'If you say so. Though Hollywood ain't above hiding the inner struggles of their money-cows,' Herb said. 'Could be she uses pills to forget that kidnapping? You remember the one, right?'

She did.

'I'm afraid I couldn't tell you, and I would ask you to refrain from spreading gossip about my guests,' Amelia replied stiffly.

Herb shrugged, then she heard the click of a shutter as he took her photo. Amelia sniffed, then lifted her chin and continued walking in silence. The insufferable journalist followed.

'Buenos dias!' she called as she neared the lighthouse. She tilted her head up to look up at the gallery deck. She'd seen Pau there earlier that day on her fateful trip down to the marina.

Seconds later, the door right in front of her lurched open and Pau himself emerged.

'Hola, Amelia,' he said with a formal bow of his head and a smooth smile. Amelia blossomed in the warmth of his greeting, then reminded herself that he had been arguing with David the day before. He was a suspect, however charming he was.

'Farero,' Amelia greeted him formally in Spanish for 'lighthouse keeper'—by far his loftiest role on the island. Then, she drew in a deep breath, readying herself to question him about his argument with David.

'I knew there was something wrong with that man. He said he was repairing his broken yacht, but I tell you, he knew nothing of engines. *Nada!*' As he spoke, Pau gesticulated with his hands and his voice rose to a crescendo.

'How do you know?'

'Because of the tractor. With that he was...how do you say it? *No serve para nada*. And now this!' He threw his hands into the air. '*¡Los inocentes no son asesinados!*'

Pau thought David was no help in fixing the tractor, and Amelia had to admit those tools laid out in neat rows on his yacht didn't scream mechanic at work. She would take a closer look when she plucked up the courage to go back to the crime scene.

David's pile of money and lack of mechanical prowess was important, she knew it. Though she could not agree with Pau that *¡Los inocentes no son asesinados.* Innocents were being murdered every day, somewhere in the world. But Pau's gut was right about David. This particular victim was, she decided, very far from innocent.

'Did you notice anything out of the ordinary between midnight and 2.30 am?'

Pau frowned, considering. 'No, nothing.' He scratched his chin, still thinking. 'I stayed on *el balcón* smoking a cigar until one. After that I went to bed... But even in my bed,' he smiled and gave her a twinkly look, 'nothing out of the ordinary occurred.'

'You heard nothing?'

'I am a very light sleeper. Even the crickets rouse me... You can be assured that I would have heard a shot from a weapon capable of *that*.' Amelia shivered in revulsion, remembering the gory results of that shot. But stomach-turning as it was, she had no reason to doubt Pau.

'You do not wish to talk of it... I understand. But it must be said that a weapon that powerful *must* make a sound!'

'Could the shot not have been muffled?'

'Anything is possible,' Pau agreed, though he looked doubtful. 'There is little doubt I would have woken, and if not me, the flamingos.' Pau nodded to himself, as if agreeing with his own theory. Case closed.

'Do you own a gun?' Amelia asked.

'*¡Que horror!*' he gasped. 'I would never! I am...how do you say...allergic to the guns!' Pau said, again gesticulating wildly with his hands, his face a picture of horror. 'I once travelled to Bosnia... All those beautiful buildings, their faces covered with bullet holes. Their graceful lines destroyed by the weapons of war. It broke *mi corazón*,' he replied, seriously.

A silencer... Amelia mused as she smiled her thanks and turned to leave. *Though we can't even tell what type of gun was used until the police arrive with their forensics.* Herb, who had been busy taking photos while no doubt listening in on their conversation, picked up a small branch and threw it for the dogs.

Intuition had Amelia pausing on the path and turning back to Pau. 'Will you join us for dinner this evening, Farero?'

'With pleasure, beautiful lady,' Pau replied as she headed back down the path, Herb and her dogs following.

As Amelia trudged the path, she considered the murder weapon again. Where on this tiny island could a murderer have found a weapon powerful enough to inflict that kind of damage to David?

She and Uncle Seb had had very different views on the hunting of wildlife. He had been a military man with little tolerance for Amelia's brand of sensitivity. She, Leo, and Daisy had watched him clean and load his weapons in preparation for his hunting expeditions. Leo might even have gone with him once or twice.

Sebastian Ferver had been something of a collector of lame ducks over the years. She could recall many a holiday where he'd been housing an old friend, or even a recent acquaintance who had fallen on hard times. It explained his initial befriending of Oliver, who at the time had just completed a tour of military service and was suffering from shellshock, which is what they now called PTSD.

Oliver never once spoke of his time in the military; his sour demeanour and competence with a first-aid kit spoke for themselves. Though there was one thing in that regard that he *was* vocal on: his opposition to Sebastian's gun collection.

Which was why, on coming to the island, Amelia had packed them up and sent them to a gun dealer in Mallorca to be sold.

She doubted the artists would be harbouring weapons in their cabins or in their gallery, for after all, hadn't they lived quietly and peacefully on this island for years? Even so, she would make sure to have a little shufty around while she was there, just to make sure.

She turned the final bend which brought the little group of buildings, huddled at the foot of the mountain, into view.

She headed for the nearest hut, which from memory belonged to Barron Lancaster. He was a successful businessman, as well as an artist. He had carefully fostered an image of himself as a tortured artist, and though he generally dressed himself up like Lord Byron—in a plum-coloured floor-length dressing gown, worn over a shirt, cravat, breaches, and knee-high riding boots—he had a whole trunk-full of costumes stored in old steam trunks which doubled up as seating if anyone came a-visiting.

The gothic image was diametrically opposed to the eight-foot high, bright-pink impressionist paintings of flamingos he was famous for. *All those layers of silk and wool must be murder in the summer heat!* Amelia thought.

It was all an act, of course. Just like his name, which she suspected he had chosen so that people might think he was a baron.

Amelia remembered Oliver once telling her, Leo, and Daisy a story about the night when Uncle Sebastian had brought Barron to the island, without warning and under the cover of darkness. Oliver and his gang of teenage irregulars had laughed as they thought up wilder and wilder theories for the secrecy of his arrival. Amelia had been certain he was some sort of criminal, while Leo and Daisy were both convinced that he was a spy. They were all proved wrong when he had begun churning out his now trademark works of flamingo impressionism.

Amelia flushed at her childhood fancies as she approached Barron, who was standing on his doorstep. At his side was Beatrice—a Parisienne mosaic artist who possessed the poised, if fragile, elegance of a movie star, even though she must have been in her fifties.

'Beatrice, Barron, it is good to see you,' Amelia greeted them warmly.

'*Bonjour, ma cherie,*' Beatrice replied as they moved down the steps to greet her, Beatrice kissing her on both cheeks and Barron offering her a little bow before draping his arm over Beatrice's shoulders.

'We 'ave 'eard your disturbing news. You and David were close?' Beatrice asked.

'Not close.' Amelia shook her head. 'In fact, I was hoping you might tell me something about him? Or whether you noticed anything unusual last night.'

'I wish I could, *cherie*. I 'ad 'eard he was a *scoundrel*, but perhaps not,' Beatrice replied, shrugging her shoulders, unmoved by events. 'As to last night, I 'ad planned to join Barron 'ere at midnight, but I misjudged the kiln. My pots were not ready,' she mourned. 'And after that, one of your guests arrived at *notre petit* camp. She was lost, the poor soul, so I of course guided her back to the path. After this, I returned *á mon amour*,' she explained, fluttering her lashes and placing her hand on Barron's forearm.

So, it looks like Maud was telling the truth.

'We play, 'ow do you say it...dress up?' Beatrice said, throwing Barron a saucy wink. Barron winced.

'Well...uh...thank you for guiding my mother back to the path, Beatrice. I can't imagine why she came this far.'

'Who knows? But I help 'er because it is right to do it. Still, we will *all* be 'appier when these talentless 'ollywood types stop creeping around in the darkness and go 'ome. Perhaps then, we will know peace once more. *Mais oui, la créativité* depends on it,' Beatrice said, still clinging to Barron's arm and gazing adoringly up at him.

'We saw nothing that would help you,' Barron said. 'I'm sorry, Amelia, but we can tell you nothing about the unfortunate death of your guest.'

'Murder. He was *murdered*,' Amelia snapped, her feathers ruffled by his lack of empathy. 'Do you have any guns?' she asked.

'I have my musket,' he replied, smiling slyly before admitting, 'It is an accessory to one of my military uniforms. A fake. Or a prop, as you actor types would say. But I would turn your gaze inward, dear.

Your uncle had a whole case full of them in the old house. Perhaps, someone got ahold of one of those?'

His words stung with accusation, but his face was placid, serene. Barron had lived on the island for almost two decades, and during that time, Amelia was ashamed to admit, she had treated him not as a person with feelings and failings, but as two-dimensional. A bit player with a non-speaking role in the adventure that was her uncle's life.

But now Amelia was seeing him clearly for the first time. Barron was a chameleon; he had turned himself into a blank canvas. She scanned his outlandish outfit, wondering if his disguises weren't the only costumes he wore. Was he also hiding his true nature? Amelia shivered, not wanting to think about what might lie beneath his millpond surface. If Barron had not had an alibi, he'd have leapt to the top of her suspect list.

'I shipped the guns off when I arrived. I have no time for them,' Amelia replied, moving away.

Herb had hung back while they were chatting, though his attention never left them. *He's plotting something to make this innocuous conversation seem salacious,* Inner-Maud warned as Amelia crossed the clearing to the shadow artist's cabin.

Oliver's Hank was the third occupant of the little encampment, the one who apparently had no use for the mundanity of a name. He suffered from something called achromatopsia, seeing everything in monochrome shades of black and grey, not colour. He didn't venture out during daylight hours as his disability caused extreme light sensitivity.

Her knock at the door was met with a low rumbling. It was a voice, but she couldn't make out the words. *Welcome, Amelia, please do come in,* Amelia imagined it to say, so she lifted the latch and walked in. A big, redheaded man was sitting on a low stool, facing an easel. He was tinkering with some paints as she approached. Herb wandered uninvited amongst the paintings hung or propped up against the walls.

The shadow artist didn't look away from his canvas as she carefully closed the door to shut out the light. The warring smell of oil paints and turpentine filled the air of the small room, almost robbing Amelia of her breath.

'I know nothing of your murder,' the big man rumbled again, though this time Amelia could make out the words. 'I was painting wildlife in the woods behind the beach all night. I was nowhere near the marina. I'm sorry I can't help you.'

Amelia didn't think he sounded particularly sorry; more abrupt and unwelcoming. *But rudeness does not a killer make.*

'Hey!' Herb exclaimed from behind her. She spun around to see him standing by a large painting. 'When did you paint our princess?' he asked.

Amelia hurried over to where he was standing. He wasn't wrong. There, in all its monochrome glory, was a painting of a tall, willowy, blonde woman. She was creeping through the trees.

'You painted this last night?' she asked.

'Yes. The light last night was perfect. Almost a full moon and it was made even more beautiful with the appearance of this nymph.'

'Did you speak to her?' Amelia asked.

He shook his head, his face a rigid mask as he swivelled on his stool to face the painting on the easel in front of him. Amelia was dismissed.

I need to talk to Daisy, Amelia thought as she left the cabin, heading across the little clearing toward the path that would take them back to the hotel.

She took one last glance over her shoulder to see Herb and Beatrice standing close together talking quietly.

'Will you join us for dinner tonight?' she asked, raising her voice.

'Oh, how kind. *À quelle heure?*' Beatrice asked.

'Is nine too late?'

'Not at all. We will look forward to it, will we not? *Adieu,*' she said, walking away from Herb to re-join Barron on the step of his cabin. Herb walked across the clearing to join Amelia, turning only briefly to tap two fingers against his head, a salute to Beatrice.

Something about that gesture...

It took a good five minutes of walking back down the path for her to remember, and when she did, she shivered like someone had walked over her grave. The stranger on the beach with David last night—the man who appeared to have been the last person to see David alive—had done the same thing.

What does it mean? Was it Herb down on the beach with David? And if so, is it possible he had followed David back to his boat and murdered him? But why?

And now that she thought about it, the salute wasn't the only evidence against Herb. Like the others, he had been affected by David's presence when they arrived, *and* he had come to reception in the middle of the night to complain about a missing lightbulb. Who does that?

Someone who needs an alibi...

Herb was rounding the corner of the building, so Amelia didn't have a chance to ask him about it then...not that she would have, not alone, not when he was now her prime suspect in David's murder.

So, instead of following him and confronting him, she went looking for Oliver. She needed to talk through the evidence with the one person on the island she knew was innocent.

'Darling!' Maud called out to her as she crossed the drawing room. She was sitting, partially hidden in a wing-backed easy chair, waiting to pounce.

Amelia was almost to the other side of the room, considered ignoring her, but stopped and waited instead.

'I need to confide in you,' Maud explained. Amelia didn't look back. She kept her eyes on the door and stayed silent. 'It's important,' Maud insisted. Amelia's whole body swayed toward the door, but she knew if Maud wanted to confide something—likely something poisonous about one of her other guests—there would be no stopping her.

'What is it, Mother? I'm busy,' she said, retracing her steps and taking a seat opposite her mother.

'It's about those passports,' Maud said.

Amelia's ears pricked. She was surprised Maud had opened *this* particular train of conversation. Amelia had rather thought she'd have to prise it out of her.

'What about them, Mother?' she asked, trying to appear casual.

'You don't fool me, girl. I know you saw my reaction,' she snapped.

'You flinched.'

'And now we all know how willing you are to suspect us all, even your mother,' she continued, ignoring Amelia's comment. 'I have decided to circumvent another unpleasant confrontation.'

'Very well,' Amelia said. 'Circumvent away.'

'The passport... Dominic Strathclere,' Maud began. 'I know that name.' Amelia's face must have shown her surprise. 'Not personally, I can assure you.'

'Then *what?*'

'Well...it seems dear Leopold advised his cronies to invest in a...what do they call it? Oh yes, a fraudulent Ponzi scheme. He vouched for the investment manager. Told his chums—including the marquess of somewhere or other—that he would trust this investment manager with his sister's virtue.' Amelia nodded; she knew what was coming, but still her heart clenched in anticipation.

'That man was...' Maud paused with the dramatic timing of a magician pulling a bouquet of paper flowers out of a top hat, then dropped the axe. 'Dominic Strathclere!'

Maud continued with faux sympathy and undisguised relish. 'I'm sure it must have been a terrible shock for dear Leo to see the cause of his downfall right here on this island he thought of as a sanctuary. Perhaps they fought. It must have been an accident—' Maud broke off at last.

A deafening silence surrounded them as Amelia reminded herself to breathe. Then, fully oxygenated, she rose to her feet and walked through reception and up the stairs, counting each and every step twice, then three times.

In...out. Amelia reminded herself as she continued to process her mother's words. Either Maud was right and Leo—who, she reminded herself, *had no alibi*—murdered David over money, or Maud was attempting to frame the man who had once been her daughter's childhood friend and, later, her boyfriend. The boyfriend Maud had already lied to in order to break them up and keep Amelia a prisoner in the sad little existence she called a life.

Her ears were ringing, and her head pounded as she absorbed the impact of the blow Maud had just delivered so heartlessly.

She hardly noticed her progress along the corridor as her thoughts swirled around Leo. He'd accepted her invitation to the island only because he was *persona non grata* in London's financial circles.

He told her his life had been ruined, so he had escaped to their childhood getaway for reprieve, only to be faced with the instrument of his destruction.

She stumbled along the corridor in search of Leo. Surely, he would convince Amelia he had not murdered David. But before she had a chance to knock on the door to his suite, she glanced through the open doorway into Daisy's room.

Daisy was lying on top of her bed, curled up in a ball. There was an open bottle of pills on her nightstand. Something about the scene had Amelia rushing across the room. She squatted down beside Daisy, grabbed one of her hands, and checked for a pulse. *Thank God!* It was there, slow and strong.

'What are you doing, Lia?' Daisy murmured, her voice reed thin and puzzled. Amelia said nothing, simply stared down into her friend's face, relief flushing her skin. Daisy's eyes were glassy, her words slurred, but she was alive.

'I thought you were dead,' Amelia said after a few moments, then immediately regretted it.

'Sorry to disappoint. Just sleeping,' Daisy said. 'I'm a light sleeper and I have nightmares.' That explained the bottle. *Sleeping pills*.

'Oh darling! I didn't mean to disturb you. I'll let you be,' Amelia said, ready to leave her friend in peace.

'Every time I close my eyes, I see his face,' Daisy said, suddenly.

'Wha—' Amelia stammered. 'Whose face do you see?'

'Why Corey Wilson's, of course. It's so funny...if there was one place, one place in the whole wide world I was sure he could not follow, it was here.'

Amelia swallowed. *Corey Wilson...the third passport!* she thought, as her friend curled even tighter in on herself.

'Who is Corey?' she asked gently.

Daisy's eyes fluttered. She was barely lucid. 'The man...the man with the key to my cage.'

'The key to your...?'

'The man who took me!' she said, voice rising then falling to almost a whisper, 'I tried getting away, so many times, but he wore the key around his neck. And he always found me. He could find me anywhere...even here on our secret island.'

Amelia gasped, thinking of the key hanging from a chain around David's neck. 'Oh Daisy, how terrible!'

'Imagine,' Daisy continued, her voice like a zombie's, devoid of emotion, 'if Maud had remembered to collect me from ballet that day, instead of drinking herself into a stupor, the boogieman never would have taken me... And all this,' she gestured at the locks on the doors and windows, 'this broken life of mine might have been different. Can you imagine that, Lia? Can you?'

Daisy's eyelids were drooping but Amelia needed to know. 'Maud was meant to collect you that day?'

'The actress, the playwright, the journalist, and the Hollywood star went into a bar. Hahaha. What a silly bunch we are...' Daisy continued, her mind wandering. '...and now my indigo dress is missing. What on earth will Cinderella wear to the ball?'

Amelia watched as Daisy sank deeper into her haze, eyes fluttering shut. There would be no more sense out of her for now. She wasn't even sure Daisy knew what she was saying or how much of it was true.

But Amelia decided to try one more thing. 'I found three passports in David's things. One of them was in the name of Corey Wilson.' She pulled the passports out of her pocket, opened passport number three, and showed it to Daisy. 'Is this the man who took you?'

Daisy screamed. It was ear-piercing, like a bad actress in a low-budget horror movie. 'Why are you harassing me? Haven't I been through enough?' she wailed, peeling herself off the bed and throwing herself against the wall.

Before Amelia had time to move, she crawled to the nightstand, grabbed the lamp off its surface and hurled it at Amelia. That too crashed against the wall. Frantic, she did the same with the matches and candle. Matches flew left and right, and the candle bounced off the wall behind Amelia's head.

But just as quickly as it came, the storm passed from Daisy, her face slackened, and she dropped to the floor like a marionette with its strings cut. Price stormed into the room, took in the ugly scene, then grabbed hold of Amelia and thrust her out of the room, slamming the door in her face.

Amelia stood there in shock. She could hear the big man on the other side of the door cooing at Daisy as she sobbed in his arms.

Amelia walked downstairs on autopilot, thinking about David. She hadn't warmed to him from the start, and now he was dead. She should feel some compassion, she supposed, but she couldn't let go of the key and the passport. She had wondered, back on the *Titanic*, what kind of man would keep an old passport. And now she thought she knew:

A man who liked to keep trophies.

A man who had revelled in the suffering he had wrought on Daisy, who kept a passport and wore a key around his neck to remind him of her torment.

But it wasn't only Daisy he had tormented.

There was Wendy, who had motive after being terrified out of her mind by a stalker; Leo, whose world had been tipped on its axis by a conman; and yes, there was Daisy, who had come face to face with her kidnapper when she arrived at the hotel the day before.

Amelia...you're getting nowhere. Just stirring a potful of supposition like ingredients in a pot.

A pot. That's right, she had mouths to feed this evening, more now she had invited Pau and the artists. She needed to replenish her fruits and vegetables from the garden. And the goats needed checking. *I know! I'll take them the scraps from lunch.*

She walked into the kitchen, grabbed her pail of scraps, and went out the back door into the garden. As she rounded the side of the hotel, with the pail hanging from her elbow, she almost bumped into Leo, who was leaning against the wall.

She lifted her pail, shaking it a little so that he could see the contents. 'Fancy coming with me to feed the goats?'

CHAPTER NINE

'The goats are sure to be on the most inaccessible part of the island and...' Amelia glanced at her watch to check the time. It read 7 pm. 'I need to be back at the hotel in an hour if I'm to have dinner on the table on time,' she said, striding up a steep path. They were almost at the summit.

'Contrary, are they?'

'Only until they see food. After that it'll be a bun fight,' Amelia replied, nodding her head to the right, where the goats appeared one by one like the Native Americans always seemed to when it was time to ambush the cowboys in the old westerns.

'We're sitting ducks!' Leo said with a laugh as the goats charged down a precariously angled sheet of grey slate, bleating at the top of their lungs. The dogs were entranced; ready for a game of chase, they ran full pelt up the slope, heading them off.

Amelia took an old gardening glove out of her pail, put it on, then began to fling the vegetable and fruit scraps on the ground around them.

They'd been chatting amiably on the ascent, about the old days. Amelia had even pointed out the gnarled old olive tree that, long ago as a nimble pre-teen, Leo had been chased up by the herd of angry Highland cattle poor old Uncle Seb had tried to settle on the island. The cattle never had got used to the heat, but the Legend of the Chase had become island lore.

So, to this point, they had spoken of nothing consequential, but Amelia needed to know if Leo was innocent. She had taken some heavy blows today, and on the way up this hill she'd had realised something important.

She was being too polite, too British, as she went about her investigation. When people clammed up or turned to attack her, she changed the subject, smoothing people's feelings like they were wrinkled tablecloths. She was a caretaker, used to smoothing Maud's rumpled emotions her whole life, but that needed to change.

She wasn't going to solve this crime, and she wasn't going to save her island, if she wasn't willing to ask the difficult questions. *Might as well start now.*

'Why didn't you tell me who David was to you?' she asked over the lump in her throat.

Leo looked left and right, as if he was looking for an escape route. Not finding one, or reconsidering, his shoulders dropped. 'Um...er... How did you know?'

'Maud.'

'Of course,' he said, nodding his head. 'London is a big city full of village gossips.'

'And if there's gossip, we both know Maud will root it out and use it for her own ends,' Amelia agreed with a sad smile.

'It wasn't David I knew, though. The man who talked me out of my own inheritance, as well as my friends' savings...*his* name was Dominic Strathclere.

'When we arrived at the hotel, after that awkward drive with Daisy acting like a marionette, and Maud like a sulky harumphing child, I had no idea my day could get any worse...but it did. Because there, chatting with your man Pau, was the ne'er-do-well who ruined me.

'I'm afraid I wasn't quite straight with you, love. The hit to my reputation is so bad, I may never be able to go back,' he finished, averting his eyes.

'Ahh...' Amelia sighed.

'I'll put my hand up to hating the man. I can see how you would think I had motive to kill him. But I swear on everything I hold dear. I swear on our friendship that I had nothing to do with his death.'

Amelia stayed silent. She *desperately* didn't want Leo to be the killer, but if he was, she wanted to know...*needed* to know. So, she wasn't going to change the subject to smooth this tablecloth. Instead, she was going to cross her fingers and send up a prayer for his innocence, while simultaneously doing what the TV sleuths did: stay quiet and give Leo enough rope to hang himself.

'And I'm not the only one with a motive. He was *stalking* Wendy. And when I was out walking before dinner, I saw that awful safari-suited paparazzo standing on a stool tampering with something over the front door of his bungalow. Strange behaviour, don't you think, love?'

Amelia nodded, letting him continue. Information was the gold standard, and she needed to hear *everything*.

'And, I know you will have noticed that I wasn't the only one in shock at seeing David. There was a distinct look of hatred on Maud's face. I wonder why that was? And then—' Leo broke off, scratching his head before turning to watch the dogs who were still hunting in the low bushes near the summit.

'And then *what?*'

'Well, I was out wandering the grounds before dinner when the flamingos tore across the sky, which made me late... Anyway, I was crossing the drawing room, heading for the dining room, when I heard voices outside on the patio.'

'Voices? Whose voices?'

'Well, it was definitely Maud. She was talking to another woman. I can't say I recognised her voice. It wasn't Daisy, though. Someone older. I'll admit that

I stopped to listen to their conversation for a few moments, precisely *because* I didn't recognise the voice.'

'What were they talking about?' Amelia asked.

'Maud said something about it not being her fault. How could *she* have known the toy boy would show up. Something like that. And the other woman said something about it being *her* life that had been ruined by that man, not Maud's. That *she* could have been somebody. Which was when I left.'

'Oh Leo! Why didn't you tell me before now?'

He shrugged. 'She's your mother, Lia. I might not like her very much just now, but—'

'*I* don't like her very much right now. She's acting secretive and it's making my skin itch. But I also don't like being lied to.'

'Lie?'

'By omission,' she seethed. 'By hampering my investigation, you great ignoramus. How can I trust you when you withhold information? I need someone in my corner, someone I can trust.' Her last words were loud—too loud for a serious sleuth—not that Leo had taken offence. While she was furious with him, he was chuckling. *Chuckling!*

'Hampering your investigation?' he snorted.

'Don't laugh at me, Leopold Alcott, or you'll regret it.'

'I'm not laughing at you, you goose. I'm laughing next to you,' he said, moving from chuckling to guffawing.

After a while, they fell into silence, both absorbing what Leo had revealed and what it might mean. They both turned around and began their descent in silence.

As they walked, Amelia spotted Sawubona and Tantriana stripping off their clothes and running laughing into the lake, not a care in the world. *Oh dear,* she thought, *I do hope Herb isn't out with his zoom lens to catch the skinny-dipping couple.* She noticed the flamingos were back to their usual selves, all that inexplicable drama from the evening before long forgotten, and down at the artists village she watched as Beatrice strolled down the path, wandered across the clearing, and entered Barron's cabin.

'I can't believe we've been up here for almost an hour,' Amelia said, removing her gaze from her watch and picking up the pace. 'I've invited Pau and the artists over for dinner. I'm expecting them at nine, and in all the upset, I haven't even mentioned it to Oliver. If I don't give him good warning, he'll be all prickly with the guests at dinner.'

Leo laughed as they entered a copse of trees and the path meandered around to the left. The trees were thick enough to shut out most of the light.

As they turned the corner, Amelia noticed something odd a few metres ahead. They both came to a dead stop.

There, slumped against Leo's gnarled old olive tree of El Pedrusco legend, half suspended from a low branch by the strap of his camera, so tightly around his neck that it was buried deep in his flesh, was Herb.

Amelia raced over to him, desperately trying to check for a pulse, though she could already see he was dead. How could he be anything else, with the skin of his face all purple and a little drizzle of blood trailing from his mouth?

Leo was quickly beside her. He grabbed Herb around the middle and hefted his body up off the ground far enough that the strap loosened. 'See if you can get him free!' he ordered.

She did as he said, tugging at the strap, but the branch broke, and Herb's whole dead weight landed on Leo. Together the two men rolled over and over, until Leo was lying on his back beneath Herb's dead body. He yelped, then pushed, rocking the body back and forth while he wriggled out from beneath it. Eventually, the two men lay side by side in the dirt. Only one of them was panting.

'He's dead,' Amelia said, legs weak. 'Another one, *dead.*'

'What should we do?' Leo asked, still catching his breath.

Amelia had no idea. She couldn't see through the tears brimming on her eyelids, but she *could* taste saliva in her mouth. *Don't be sick, Lia.*

The sickness passed, replaced by an inner voice that screamed at her to turn tail and run, and to keep on running until everything that had happened over the past two days was nothing but a distant memory in her rear-view mirror. But she couldn't do that. Not with poor Herb dead at her feet and the rest of her guests in mortal danger. No, she would zip her emotions up inside her, like she would zip up an old anorak, and she would not unzip that anorak until she had learned everything she could from Herb's body and this crime scene. *I can fall apart in the privacy of my suite.*

But Amelia, there's a bloody killer on this island! Inner-Maud wailed. *Turning tail and running is utterly reasonable. No one would judge you for it.*

I know there's a killer, Mother! And if you'd just shut up for a moment, maybe I can work out who it is.

Surprisingly, Inner-Maud complied. Amelia took a moment to recover herself, practicing some deep breathing.

'Was he warm?' Amelia asked. 'He can't have been there long. That branch was barely strong enough to hold him.'

Leo shuddered. 'Yes. Warm.'

'And he wasn't here when we walked up this path less than an hour ago,' she said.

'No, I think we'd have noticed that,' Leo quipped, although neither of them smiled. This was not the time for smiles.

'It means time of death is within the last hour, say between 7 and 8 pm, and more importantly, I now have *two* people on the island, other than myself, with solid alibis for at least one murder. You, and Oliver, who was being his usual workaholic self when David was murdered.' Amelia, who felt cold seeping into her bones, as was her wont, began to consider the numbers. Numbers were solid, predictable, and they never lied.

'Yesterday afternoon there were fifteen people on the island. Then David was murdered, followed by...' she waved her arm towards Herb without looking at him again. 'Which leaves thirteen. Of those thirteen there are three with alibis. Oliver...you...and me. Which leaves us with ten suspects, if you don't count the goats or the flamingos.' She was thinking aloud. *Why am I so cold? Why am I talking about goats?* she wondered. *And why is Leo squinting his eyes at me?*

Amelia's eyes filled with tears of horror...and of relief. At last, she had an ally she could trust.

Not that she didn't trust Oliver. Of course, she knew she could trust him, but he was like an old rheumatic dog; volatile, even a little unstable, from pain. You must always be on guard with a dog like that.

But Leo, he was a different matter. He was more like Chessie, full of fun and exuberance, but he was also predictable in all the best ways. His optimism and his stability would make him a perfect sidekick.

'What now?' Leo asked, breaking into Amelia's thoughts, reminding her she was standing right beside a dead person and taking no action. That wouldn't do.

'You run down and get Oliver and his trusty tarp. I'll wait here and search for clues.'

'Are you sure you'll be okay here on your own, love?'

'Yes, whoever did this is long gone. Herb wasn't a random murder. There was method to this, and I have no reason to believe I'm on a death list.' Amelia wasn't sure if it was Leo she was trying to reassure or herself. Either way, it worked—Leo shot her a tiny smile and turned away, and she breathed a little deeper, her equilibrium restored.

Amelia knelt by the body and gingerly began searching Herb's pockets. His chest pocket held his paparazzi pad. She moved to his shorts pockets where she found a wallet bulging with money. There was a lump in the leather on one side of the wallet, and when she wriggled her fingers inside, she found a folded piece of paper. Unfolding it, she realised it was a photograph; a family portrait of a man, a woman, and a child. It was old and discoloured. The man and woman were so opposite they reminded Amelia of Jack Sprat and his wife from the old nursery rhyme. The age of the photograph and the man's resemblance to Herb made Amelia's heart clench.

It was his family. Were his parents dead, or would they live a parent's worst nightmare of surviving their only child? She refolded the photograph and tucked it back into his wallet.

That was all he had on him, so she stood up and studied the crime scene. She could picture Herb lurking in the bushes, as he had been when Amelia had bumped into him earlier. She could imagine someone creeping up behind him, grabbing hold of his camera strap and throttling him with it. That seemed plausible.

She dropped to her hands and knees to search the area around the body. *Most undignified,* sniffed Inner-Maud as she searched diligently, crawling in straight lines up and down the small clearing, as if she was mowing a lawn.

Nothing! But after a few minutes Chessie came galloping out of the undergrowth with a captain's hat hanging from his mouth. *Yes! Like Leo, Chessie makes a perfect sidekick,* Amelia thought, grabbing the hat out of his slobber-filled mouth before slowly retracing his steps, moving away from the path into the deeper brush.

Her heart beat faster when, not far from the path, maybe five feet or so, she found another clue: a strip of indigo fabric. Indigo fabric she had seen before.

Panting voices carried on the breeze. *Leo is back with Oliver.* Looking around one more time and seeing nothing, she hurried back out into the little clearing to find Oliver and Leo rolling the body onto a tarp. *What a boy scout!* Amelia thought. But with Oliver's reassuring childhood-grazed-knee-swabbing presence just feet away, her resolve to remain zipped up and emotionless until she reached her room dissolved. The tragic reality of her day, and the memory of Herb's photograph of a smiling family, hit her.

Two men were dead. There was no avoiding that truth, not with Oliver and Leo manhandling this second body into a tarp right at her feet. Amelia let out a sob.

Oliver and Leo looked up just as her sleuth façade cracked. 'Take her back,' Oliver ordered before continuing his work with the tarp and thick orange twine.

Leo nodded, then hurried over to her, wrapped an arm around her shoulders, and began guiding her down the path towards the hotel.

'Why...*now*?' Amelia asked.

'Shush,' Leo ordered gruffly. 'We'll sort all this out. Don't you worry.'

His arm around her felt good; *right*. The warmth of him flowed through her, stealing the chill from her bones.

'I'm better. It was just such a shock,' she began to explain, just as she spotted Maud. She was running towards them, up the path. Her lips were moving, and her face was contorted in horror. She was shouting something and waving her arms in the air, but Amelia couldn't make out the words. Not until she had covered half the distance between them.

'Daisy is missing!' Maud screeched as she thundered up to them and almost ploughed through them in her haste.

'When Leo told us the news, everyone gathered in the drawing room. Two men dead...someone picking us off one by one...we felt safer together.' She was gasping for breath, doubled over with her hands on her knees.

'Someone noticed that Daisy wasn't with us. I'm not sure...it might have been me,' she said. 'We decided to split up to look for her. I searched the ground floor—my hips ache so in this humidity. Price looked upstairs, while Wendy ran around to the bungalows. Daisy was nowhere to be found... She's completely disappeared!'

CHAPTER TEN

All her guests were running around the drawing room like clucking hens in a panic when Amelia and Leo arrived back at the hotel. As Maud had said, the guests were sticking together like glue.

'If we're all together, we can't get murdered,' was Price's simple theory, though he clearly hadn't watched any classic British whodunnits, where the murderer always found a way to pick off his prey one gruesome slaying at a time.

After Amelia's 'swoon'—his words, not hers—Leo had insisted on escorting her to a comfy chair. 'Get her a drink, someone,' Leo ordered, gently removing her sparse collection of clues—the captain's hat and the strip of fabric—from her hands and placing them on the nearby coffee table.

Amelia couldn't deny she'd had a wobble. She was feeling much better now, although she was still confused about Herb; she'd been sure he was the murderer. Anyway, she wished Leo would stop treating her like an invalid.

'Don't be such a fusspot,' she said. 'I can't sit around twiddling my thumbs! Not only do I have a missing person to locate and two murders to solve, I also need to talk to Oliver about dinner. He has no idea we have extra guests tonight,' she said, trying to rise to her feet.

'Stay where you are,' Leo ordered, his voice firm but his hands gentle as he guided her back into the wing chair. 'At least, have a drink and reorientate yourself before you start caretaking the rest of us.'

'Five minutes. Not a second longer,' Amelia capitulated with a sigh, accepting a glass of something golden brown from her mother. Moving away, Maud noticed the items on the table.

'Why in heaven's name are you carrying around a scrap of fabric?' she asked, picking it up and running it through her hands. 'It looks like it could have been torn from one of Daisy's gowns.'

Like all movie stars, Daisy had a dresser and a stylist who had perfected her 'look.' And Maud was right, that satin was just her style. *What do you mean it's just her style?* snapped Inner-Maud. *We both know that is the exact dress Price delivered to her suite yesterday.*

'And now she's missing,' Price said, gloomily.

A frisson spread through the room. Daisy was missing. An item that looked like it belonged to her was found at the crime scene. And she had motive; not that Amelia had told them *that*, but even if they didn't *know*, by the looks on their faces, they *knew*.

'Hold on,' Amelia said. 'We can't go making accus—'

'If it isn't her, why has she run?' Maud interrupted.

'I'm the first to admit the girl hasn't been herself on this trip, but Daisy wouldn't whip a mule if it crapped in her stilettos! Not an ounce of violence in that girl,' Price said, though his pallor said otherwise.

Amelia ran her hands down her face, trying to think.

Last night, I saw someone leaving the hotel in a red dress, not indigo.

But her party dress was that exact shade. You saw it with your own eyes! Inner-Maud reminded her.

Which she told us was missing! Amelia hissed back.

An elaborate plan! You can't pretend she didn't have motive to kill David...and now she's disappeared, said Inner-Maud, insistent on getting the last word, as usual.

Amelia knew if she told her guests about Daisy's link to David's alter-ego, Corey, they would instantly condemn her. But, like Price, Amelia couldn't bring herself to believe it. Her childhood playmate. A girl who wouldn't squish a mosquito that was gleefully turning her into a pin cushion. *No, I will not believe it. But I must find her so she can explain things herself.*

She glanced down at the two items on the table. Where did the captain's hat figure into all of this?

Amelia was already on her feet, ready to begin her search, when Oliver appeared in reception. Once again, he was accompanied by Pau. The two men shuffled past the reception desk and through the door that led to the kitchen, poor Herb's limp body suspended between them.

'Oh, Oliver!' Amelia cried, rushing into the kitchen after them. The freezer door was open, so Amelia carefully averted her eyes while they hoisted Herb into it, only opening them when she heard the heavy door slam shut.

'Daisy is missing, and our guests are turning themselves inside out in their efforts not to call her a murderer,' Amelia said.

'If she's missing, why aren't you combing the hotel for her?' Oliver asked, always a man of action.

Amelia growled. 'I only just got free of Leo playing mother hen. I thought you might like to help me look,' Amelia said. 'Oh, and by the way, Pau and the artists are joining us for dinner.' Oliver scowled over at Pau, who had apparently failed to mention dinner during the second crime scene clearance of the day.

'And what delights, may I ask, do you plan on feeding the five thousand?' Oliver enquired haughtily, though Amelia was saved from defending herself when Leo poked his head around the door.

'Need any help in here?' he asked.

Rolling his eyes, Oliver beckoned him into the room. 'Pau, you check the marina, the lighthouse, and the artists' community, then come back here for dinner...which will be a little later than planned,' he ordered, then gave Amelia a look. 'And be careful. We don't know anything for sure. Do we, dear?'

Amelia looked away and scowled as Pau gave Oliver a little bow then rushed out of the room.

'Leo, you check the outdoor terraces and gardens, as well as the guest bungalows,' Oliver continued.

'On it,' he said, racing out the back door.

'Amelia, check the bedrooms while I search all the downstairs rooms. And remember, there *is* a killer out there, so be careful. Meet me back here in half an hour, without fail.'

Amelia had to ask. 'You don't really think Daisy could have done it, do you?'

'Like I said, we don't know *anything* for sure. Now go.'

Amelia could admit to being a little disgruntled at the takeover, but instead of lambasting him, she gave him a cursory nod before going off to search the bedrooms.

Amelia began preparing the dinner after a fruitless investigation of the bedrooms. As her hands moved, chopping and peeling, slicing and dicing, she reviewed the situation.

Two people had been murdered, they were stranded on El Pedrusco with no way to contact the police until her guests started arriving, and her childhood best friend, who some might consider the prime suspect, was nowhere to be found. *Oh, Uncle Sebastian, what were you thinking!*

'You do realise that by disappearing, Daisy has become our prime suspect,' Oliver announced as he stalked into the kitchen far later than the allotted half hour.

'Or maybe she's already our next victim. Did you consider that, Oliver?' Amelia asked, chop-chop-chopping the salad in agitation. This was why Leo made a much better sidekick than Oliver. Leo wouldn't point out unpalatable truths, because Leo had a pure soul who saw the best in people. Oliver was a different matter altogether.

There was a commotion from the drawing room and, hoping it might be Daisy returning unharmed, Amelia was through the swing doors before her knife hit the chopping board.

It was not Daisy. Instead, standing near the window with Price, Wendy, and Leo—as well as the island's other residents: Pau, Barron, and the shadow artist, Hank—were Beatrice Besson and Maud. The shadow artist was wearing wraparound sunglasses and a strange cacophony of mismatched clothing in clashing colours. He busied himself by pulling the heavy curtains closed to shut out the last rays of sun. Maud had hold of Beatrice's upper arm in a tight grip and was glaring daggers at her. They were mid-quarrel while everyone else in the room stood frozen.

Beatrice had the back of her hand pressed against her forehead, her face contorted as tears rolled down her face.

Why me? What did I ever do to deserve a mother who could make Genghis Khan cry?

Amelia approached them and stood, hands on hips, until her mother noticed her.

Maud opened her mouth to speak but was interrupted by Beatrice who violently snatched her arm out from Maud's grip, stumbled the last few steps to Amelia, and threw herself weeping, into her arms. 'Pau came to us... He told us—' she faltered, swallowing hard to regain her composure. 'He told us Daisy is missing, and I'm afraid it is all my fault!' She collapsed, sliding through Amelia's arms into a stylish, sobbing heap on the floor.

People were rushing about, picking Beatrice up off the floor, helping her to a seat, bringing her a drink, all while Amelia's mind spun like a scratched record. It suddenly made sense.

This sobbing woman was the key to Maud's secrets. Her mother had acted weird around David the moment she'd clapped eyes on him, and Amelia was certain her mother had also recognised Beatrice in the yoga room. Finally, Leo told her he'd overheard Maud speaking to someone outside the dining room the previous evening. *Could Beatrice be the other woman?*

If she was, Amelia was anxious to find out what they had been discussing. First, she wanted to hear what Beatrice thought was all her fault.

As if on cue, Beatrice groaned, coming round from her faint.

'I must tell you! I cannot keep it to myself any longer,' Beatrice said, shuffling up on the chaise to an upright position.

'My name,' she said, articulating the words now in a plummy English accent, 'is not Beatrice Besson, but Violet Forrester... You may recognise my name,' she said, her gaze moving from guest to guest. Amelia's knees wobbled at the name. 'I was an accomplished actress in my own right...before my career was *ruined.*'

She seemed to grow in stature, sitting straighter as she embodied the persona of Violet Forrester. But Amelia barely noticed; she was still absorbing the shock.

Violet Forrester was Daisy's mother.

The same mother who had been visibly broken when her daughter was snatched off the street, but who, on hearing that her daughter had been found, hadn't even waited around for her return before disappearing herself. *And how is it that this bad penny has turned up here on my island in the middle of a murder case?*

Amelia took a seat in a chair not far from Violet, trying to comprehend this new truth. She had known Violet Forrester as a child, but the woman in front of her bore little resemblance. When she and

Daisy had lived around the corner from one another in London, they'd been teenagers. Back then, Violet had looked just like her daughter did now—a tall willowy blonde with charisma in spades and enough clout to have the metropolitan police out in their droves, searching for the daughter of cinematic royalty.

But Violet's hair was darker now, somewhere between auburn and full redhead. She'd kept her waiflike figure, though her outlandish flowing garment made it hard to tell. And she must have had some minor plastic surgery in the years since she'd been missing. Her cheekbones were more prominent than the Violet Amelia knew, and her famous pert nose, the starlet's single most identifiable attribute, had been moulded into a longer, slenderer beak. The transformation was astonishing, which left Amelia with a confusing smorgasbord of questions.

'Can you explain to me how you think this is your fault?' Amelia asked gently.

Beatrice...no *Violet* gave a long, slow blink before explaining. 'It starts, I suppose, with how I raised her. Spare the rod and spoil the child, as they say,' Violet said, stiffening her shoulders. 'She ran amok after her father took that job in Hollywood and left us an ocean away in London. She was too much for me to handle alone.'

'But how does that make all this your fault?' Leo asked, frowning.

'Oh...I suppose it doesn't. But the sheer *wilfulness,* the absolute *spitefulness* of the girl, took its toll on me, and I was forced into the arms of my co-star. You remember, don't you, Maud?'

'Oh, I remember alright,' Maud replied. 'I was staging a play in the West End. I had cast Violet in the lead role, opposite an up-and-coming young actor—'

'Corey,' Amelia interrupted, eyes wide with understanding.

Violet nodded. 'Corey was the cause of my downfall. The boy was beautiful, and he positively oozed charm from every pore. It never got as far as him meeting Daisy, but nevertheless, I thought what we had together was special... But when Daisy was kidnapped, just when I needed him most, Corey disappeared,' Violet said, staring at her hands clasped in her lap. She was twisting a tissue between her fingers, as if strangling it.

'And then the rumours began. Rumours that he was involved in some way—a kidnapper! The idea was hideous.' Violet swallowed as she continued to shred the tissue in her hands. 'Then came the whispers, the paparazzi, the damned magazines! They asked, no they *suggested* in their headlines that I might have something to do with it! "Where was Violet Forrester when her poor daughter was taken?" Questions were asked, I couldn't shake the press, and I decided to leave London for good.'

Amelia remembered it much the same, but the state of Daisy's mother had been the least of her worries then.

'You may judge me now, but how could I face my fans with the smear of *his* crime on my reputation?' With tears rolling down her cheeks, she begged for understanding. 'As soon as I heard Daisy was safe—before she even returned—I ran. I'm not proud of it, but I...' She broke off, dabbing her eyes. 'Daisy was sent to live with her father in Hollywood. She was better off without me, wasn't she? She built a castle on the bedrock of that notoriety. She thrived!'

Amelia gasped. Was Daisy's own mother accusing her of capitalising on what happened to her?

'And then, a month ago, I was delivering my daily offering to the shrine when I glimpsed a man who resembled Corey. I couldn't be sure it was him—I had not seen his face for close to fifteen years—and I have spent so many years hiding myself away that it was natural for me to stay in the shadows.'

'You didn't approach him?' Amelia asked.

'No. I thought it best to keep my distance. Then that ship sailed into our harbour and *ta-da*...my daughter stepped off it. I didn't know what to do.'

'Staying hidden is what you did,' Oliver whispered from behind Amelia's shoulder.

'I couldn't quite decide if this coming together might be a blessing. Either Daisy would not recognise Corey, because he had not been involved in the kidnapping, or she would, and the truth would come out.' Violet's gaze was intense as it rested on Amelia.

'But I still don't understand how it's your fault,' Amelia said, not to be swayed by the drama.

'Don't you see? I knew from her father that Daisy was unstable. I should have known if she recognised Corey that she would lose her mind and take her revenge! It was a powder keg... Oh dear, if only I had *said* something.'

'Are you saying you believe Daisy killed David?' Amelia asked, leaning forward.

'I... I just don't know,' Violet faltered, confused. 'All I know is I placed her in this position, and if anyone is to blame, it's me. I'm so sorry Amelia, I know how important this weekend is to you.'

There was a rumble of agreement from the occupants of the room. On top of Daisy's own mother's suspicions, the scrap of fabric from the scene of Herb's murder was right there in front of them.

'It doesn't make any sense,' Leo interrupted.

Ah-ha! One person who isn't just lapping it up!

'Why would she kill Herb? There's no way he could have known about Daisy's history with David.'

'Why, my dear boy,' Violet replied, 'Herb Hogan, the king of the Hollywood press pack, was a lowly fleet street journalist fifteen years ago. He covered the case for one of the tabloids. I even granted him an interview if I remember correctly.

'There is no doubt in my mind that he would have known the story. What if he knew more about the case than the rest of us? What if he knew who Corey was and what he did? When Corey was killed, I can only imagine—with his bloodhound's nose for a story—that he approached Daisy with what he knew.'

Amelia wanted to doubt her story, but Violet's anguish looked genuine.

'Sandwiches, anyone?' Amelia croaked, though the boulder had grown so large inside her she could barely choke out the words. 'It's far too late to cook.'

Half an hour later, they were scattered around the drawing room, heaping plates full of hummus salad sandwiches balanced precariously on their laps.

'Of course, it is devastating that two men have been killed,' Maud slurred, polishing off her third scotch. 'Daisy must be found, but as you can see, you have guests who *have* survived, and at least one of them would like to finish whatever this is that you have served up in place of a proper dinner and then find somewhere safe so she can get some much-needed sleep.'

Of course, Maud would go there. *Never let it be said that my mother would show compassion in the face of sorrow,* Amelia thought ruefully. But Maud wasn't finished. 'Surely, we should just wait for the Commissioner of Police, or whatever he calls himself, to arrive and commence his investigations?'

'Mother! You know as well as I do that nothing looks good for Daisy. We must be certain it really was her *before* the police arrive. They will arrest her just because she's the obvious suspect,' Amelia argued.

'Is that it, *daughter?* Or is it because you will lose everything if the girl is not here for the gala on Saturday?' Maud replied, an edge of derision in her voice. Scotch never did improve her demeanour.

Amelia felt the heat rise from her chest and rest between her two temples. She breathed, felt her temperature cool, then looked at the rest of the room. 'Two men have been murdered. I've done all I can do to create something I hoped you would all enjoy, but if I lose it, then so be it. It's not more important than the truth. The rest of Daisy's life could very well be in the balance.'

Maud harrumphed, swirled her glass, and shot back the rest of her scotch. 'Then what, pray tell, do you suggest?'

Everyone sat in silence, waiting for Amelia to respond.

It was time. She was done with pussyfooting around.

'Oliver,' she said, choosing an ally for her first foray. 'You have an alibi for David's murder, but for the record,' she continued, and he raised his eyebrows and smirked, 'can you tell me where you were this evening between seven and eight?'

'That's easy. Pau and I were out clearing the road. We are still planning a gala, are we not?'

'Thank you, Oliver. And you Wendy?' she asked. Wendy was sitting by the window in the reading nook. She didn't resemble her normal flustered self at all. She was leaning back, legs crossed, plate expertly balanced as she munched away at a doorstop sandwich. She finished her mouthful before speaking.

'Can you believe I was having a perfectly polite conversation with your mother? Apparently, there is a job opening she would like me to consider.' Amelia grinned. It seemed Wendy had come out of her shell. David's death had been a welcome relief for her. Amelia didn't doubt poor Wendy would have been desperate enough to kill, but she had no access to a weapon and now she had an alibi for Herb's murder.

Which meant Leo, Oliver, Pau, Wendy, and Maud all had alibis. She had also spotted Sawubona and Tantriana out at the lake, which left Price, Barron, the shadow artist, and Violet...and Daisy.

'Violet, I saw you leaving the shrine room this afternoon around four, and again near your chalet as we descended the mountain a little before eight. Can you tell me where you were in between?'

'I was at the community *cre-a-ting*,' she replied, emphasising each syllable. 'I fired my kiln...then I painted some pots—or I might have used my wheel—while I was monitoring the kiln. I never leave it unattended. Dear Sebastian made me promise after a slight mishap in the early days.'

'And I'm to take your word for it?' Amelia asked.

'I should think so, but you are welcome to visit my studio; the bisque-fired pots are ready to be glazed before their second firing.'

'And Barron? Mr...umm... Can you recall where you were?' Amelia asked the other two artists.

Barron, who had been like a tennis spectator, transferring his attention from person to person as they spoke, now sat frowning into space. 'I was at the lake, painting. The monk and his muse can vouch for me. They were frolicking in the shallows, scaring away the birds,' Barron said.

'He speaks true,' Sawubona said, and Tantriana nodded her bowed head.

'I was in my cottage,' said the shadow artist. 'I do not venture outside until the sun has retreated.' *Weird place to live if you are afraid of a little sun*, Amelia thought.

'And you, Mr Whitney. Can you tell us where you were when Herb was murdered between seven and eight?'

'Beach.'

'Beach?'

'Yes. I was on the beach topping up my tan. Only useful thing I could do while we're trapped in this godforsaken place. Someone must have seen me,' he said, peering from guest to guest.

Silence. Then Amelia heard Oliver snicker. He'd clamped his hand over his mouth, like a child, by the time she swung her head round to look at him.

'Oh, alright. I saw him flopping around in the water at around seven while I was working with Pau.'

'Pau?' Amelia prompted.

'Per'aps? I believe, yes but I cannot be sure,' he said, shrugging his shoulders.

As she suspected, they all had an alibi. Which meant someone was lying or Daisy really did it. Herb certainly didn't hang himself.

But what of Maud's odd behaviour? She had recognised David but had kept it secret. Her nocturnal wanderings were Violet's alibi for that night, and now that Violet had revealed herself, were they supposed to believe the two had not recognised each other? Or...

'Mother, who were you talking to out on the terrace before dinner last night?' Amelia asked.

'What? I don't know what you're—' Maud began.

'It was me,' Violet interrupted. 'Maud had recognised me, just as she had recognised Corey. There's no need to protect me, Maud.'

Maud's face turned into a sneer, but she grudgingly explained herself. 'When they both disappeared after Daisy's kidnapping, I suspected Corey and Violet had run away together. So, after seeing Corey in the driveway when we arrived, I was on the lookout for Violet. I know she looks quite different now, but don't you see? I only recognised her because I was *expecting* to see her, whereas, after her, uh...*alterations*, and after so much time, Violet would have been unrecognisable to you. When she was here too, I thought they might still be together.' She swallowed. 'Apparently I was wro—'

'Dear Sebastian swooped in and saved me. He could not bear to see me suffer!' Violet interrupted again. 'You don't know the difficulty I faced all those years ago. How could any of *you* understand what it's like to live under the constant scrutiny and surveillance of the British press? Sebastian was my lifeline; my *angel*.'

Amelia caught Leo rolling his eyes as he said, 'How can any of this matter? We all have alibis for Herb's murder.'

'Like it or not, the clues do all seem to point to one person,' Oliver muttered.

'Who else can it be, but the girl?' Barron asked.

'The *actriz* is the killer. Of that I am certain,' Pau agreed.

But Amelia's thoughts were stuck on Sebastian and his *swooping in* to save Violet. It didn't fit.

Oh yes, Sebastian Ferver was fully prepared to rescue his loved ones…but Violet? No, Amelia knew her uncle could have easily borne Violet's suffering on his conscience. If he truly had swooped, protecting Daisy's mother was categorically not the reason.

'All that remains is for us to find my poor broken child,' Violet said, breaking into Amelia's thoughts. 'We will have to hand her over to the police, but after all she went through at the hands of that beast, I am sure they will be lenient.'

'I'm sure they will,' agreed Oliver.

'*Sí sí*, the Spanish justice system *es justo*,' Pau assured them.

CHAPTER ELEVEN

Amelia was alone at last.

She sat in the drawing room, shrouded in darkness, her ears ringing as she considered just how many of her guests had reason to hate David. Leo, because he had been swindled, Wendy, because of the stalking, and Violet, Daisy and even Maud because of that terrible kidnapping that altered all their lives all those years ago.

On the evidence, however, it looked like only Daisy, and perhaps the shadow artist—though *he* seemed to have no axe to grind with either of their victims—had not even a whiff of an alibi for Herb's murder, which had been carried out in daylight when most of the island's residents had been together. And, come to think of it, the shadow artist couldn't go out in the daylight...

Even the clue she found near Herb's body pointed to Daisy. But Amelia's acid stomach told her something didn't ring true.

'Still here?' Leo asked from the doorway.

'Yes,' Amelia replied, her voice small.

'What answers did your questions get you, love?'

'We both know everything points to Daisy, but I can't believe it.'

Leo nodded as he crossed the room and lay down on the sofa opposite her. 'Would it help to brainstorm?'

'Perhaps... Where would we start?'

'How about we walk through everyone's movements. We were all together at dinner and then afterward, until Daisy got woozy, and Herb saw her up to bed.'

'Daisy seemed drunk or stoned,' Amelia pointed out.

'Yes, which would make it difficult for her to navigate to the marina and murder David,' Leo mused. 'Anyway, onwards... We finished our game of bridge after she went to bed. Sawubona turned out to be a card shark which ended up in me winning against Oliver for the first time in my life. We chatted for a few minutes, and then Sawubona and Tantriana went off to salute something or other.'

Amelia nodded. 'Wendy went with them, remember? And you followed on soon after. Oliver and

I cleared up the mess from dinner, then headed to the office. I saw Price and Maud turn in around then.'

'So far so good,' Leo encouraged. 'What happened then?'

'I popped upstairs to change for my swim, and while I was on the landing, I spotted someone sneaking down the back staircase. The person had a dress made of fabric that looked a lot like that, only scarlet,' she said, pointing to the scrap of indigo cloth on the table.

You know it was Daisy, Inner-Maud whispered.

Leo's eyebrows raised at that new titbit of information. 'Then what?'

'Then on my way down for a swim, I saw David and what I thought was a stranger on the beach, arguing. But I don't think it was a stranger after all. I think it was Herb.'

'What? Why Herb?'

'Well, he did this two-fingered-salute gesture when they parted. I saw him do it again today. I thought it meant he was our murderer until...'

'What did you do after your swim?' Leo asked.

'I scooped up an exhausted Oliver and we both headed upstairs to our rooms.'

'Okay. So that's what we know about everyone's movements for the evening. What about during the night? During the time when David was murdered?' Leo asked.

'Well yes, that's just it. Herb came into reception complaining that there was no lightbulb on his porch. Oliver helped him out, but I swear those bungalows were checked and rechecked fifty times before you arrived.'

'That *is* strange. I can see why you suspected him. Anything else?'

'Not really. Just tantric sex noises and a rainstorm. In the morning, I came down to breakfast to a bandaged Oliver. He had cut himself cleaning up glass outside and I wondered.'

'What did you wonder, Lia?' Leo asked.

'I wondered if Herb had removed the bulb and broken it – maybe deliberately or maybe accidentally when he was stubbing out a cigarette. It would have been so neat!' she cried in frustration.

'So, that's what he was doing on that stool out on his porch,' Leo said excitedly. 'But then he went and got himself murdered.' His shoulders slumped.

'Yes. My prime suspect not only had an alibi, but then was himself murdered. It's infuriating,' Lia growled. 'Heavens, but it's wonderful to be able to confide in you.'

Leo nodded and grinned, reminding her of the nine-year-old boy she'd first met at Friday night drama class with old Madame Bellamy in Queens Gate. He'd been the only boy among twenty budding Elizabeth Taylors—each one throwing hissy fits greater than the last—which, come to think of it, might have been one of the reasons for the grin.

'Which brings us back to where we started. We need to talk to Daisy,' Amelia said, heaving in a heavy breath.

'But how?' Leo asked.

'We've known Daisy for more than two decades, since we were little kids. I just can't believe she had it in her to kill one man, let alone two.'

'I don't know.' Leo shrugged. 'Who knows what unspeakable things Dominic—er, *Corey*—did to Daisy? Perhaps things that have stayed with her for half a lifetime. I have to wonder if I might have committed murder if I was in her place,' he said. 'But I trust your gut, Lia. You always have been so much cleverer than me.'

'You got that right,' she replied with a playful, tired wink. 'Then you'll help me find her?'

Instead of replying, Leo grabbed her hand and tugged her over to the door.

What followed was hours of fruitless search. *If I'd have brought a broom with me, this place would sparkle like Cinderella's castle.* Amelia was almost too tired to go on. It was two in the morning, her back ached, and she had blisters forming on her feet.

'We've looked *everywhere*,' Leo grumbled. 'Where else can she be?'

'What about the bungalows?'

'I looked there this afternoon. They were all locked up, windows and doors shuttered.'

They stood silently facing one another. Then Amelia asked, 'Even Herb's?'

'Yes,' Leo replied.

'Herb's bungalow *shouldn't* be shuttered,' Lia said in frustration as she hurried out the back door. 'Not when it was occupied. She must be there!'

Together they ran across the back terrace, down the path to Herb's bungalow. Leo was right—the shutters were closed. But, as she approached, even in the darkness Amelia could see that they weren't locked, just pulled shut.

'She's here!' Amelia whispered, quietly pulling open the door and creeping inside. There was a small lobby with a bathroom to the left and a tiny kitchen on the right. Both were shrouded in darkness. Ahead was the doorway into the bedroom. The door was open a crack and there was a chink of light shining through. Amelia reached out and pushed the door open with the tips of her fingers.

Her heart gave a little jerk. There, lying on the bed, surrounded by papers and journals, with David's battered briefcase on the floor beside her, lay Daisy.

Amelia tiptoed across the room and crouched down beside her. Daisy's skin was pale, dark circles painted around her eyes, but she was breathing. Tears filled Amelia's eyes as she gazed down at her sleeping friend.

After a moment, Amelia gathered the papers surrounding Daisy. Underneath a small stack of papers, she found a revolver. In horror, she reached out one hand to take hold of it. It was cold and about as heavy as an iron.

She must have made a sound, because one minute she was crouched by the bed, and the next second, a torch flew past her head and crashed against the wall. Then the screeching, tear-soaked girl launched herself at Amelia who found herself lying flat on her back with Daisy sitting on top of her, one hand wrapped around Amelia's throat and the other clasping a hardback black journal with the red spine. She had it raised over her head, ready to smash down on Amelia's head.

'Daisy, no!' Amelia croaked, raising both her hands, pointing the gun at her friend. They froze; both women with arms raised, weapons in hand.

Thankfully Amelia didn't have to pull the trigger because Leo was across the room in seconds. He grabbed hold of Daisy by her raised arm and twisted it behind her back. But even that didn't stop Daisy's uncontrolled rage. She kept fighting, screaming, and writhing around, trying to break free.

Amelia scuttled backwards on her bum, stashing the gun behind her while Leo contained the distraught Daisy. 'We'll get no sense out of her now,' Amelia panted.

'I'll take her to Oliver,' Leo said, manoeuvring her out of the room, using his body to steer her.

'Be careful...and don't let go of her. We might not find her again if we lose her. She needs help,' she said, climbing to her feet and running her hands down her body, half straightening her clothes and half checking to make sure she was in one piece. 'Something in those papers pushed her over the edge of reason. I have to find out what it is.' She picked up the gun and slid it into the briefcase, then began gathering the papers and journals together. Amelia's hands were shaking uncontrollably.

'Are you sure we shouldn't get what information we can now, love?' Leo asked. His eyes were fiercer than Amelia had ever remembered. Fierce and worried.

Amelia shook her head and let out a pained breath. 'We'd have no luck talking to her now; she's too far gone. She might be calmer in the morning.'

Leo nodded sadly. Had his faith in Amelia's gut vanished after Daisy's violent outburst? Not that she blamed him. 'Okay, well don't you worry about Daisy. Oliver and I will take good care of her,' he said. Daisy had fallen nearly limp in his arms now. 'You get this cleared up and get some rest. You look dead on your feet, old girl.'

Amelia returned his nod as he dragged Daisy out of the room. It was something she never expected to see in her wildest imagination. She tried to push the ugly scene from her mind so she could focus on what mattered.

Daisy was distraught and angry this afternoon, but not violent...or at least she wasn't feral. And she didn't pull a gun on me. What's the betting that gun was used to murder David?

The question was, how did the revolver and the journals come to be in Herb's room? The answer could, of course, be that Daisy had taken them from the yacht when she murdered David, then moved them to Herb's room after she'd murdered him.

She sighed, picking up the heavy briefcase and lugging it back to her room. She was bone tired, and she certainly didn't have all the answers, but she was becoming more and more certain that something in those papers held the answer to the mystery. *I'm going to have to read every word.*

Amelia had sat in bed, flanked by her sleeping hounds, reading those wretched journals until the wee hours.

Most of them were filled with neat, handwritten notes dealing with the practicalities of abducting and ransoming a fifteen-year-old girl. Every word was a sledgehammer blow. Amelia had barely managed to keep down her sandwich as she read every word and scoured every line for a clue.

Why didn't I try harder to contact Daisy after the rescue?

Self-involved, selfish, you name it, Inner-Maud replied.

Inner-Maud was right, she thought gloomily, snuggling Tulip closer to her for comfort.

The journals proved beyond a shadow of doubt that Corey was a monster.

By the time she found one short entry, scrawled right at the bottom of the last page of one of the journals written around the time of the kidnapping—a page with the corner folded down—the tears were flowing down her cheeks unchecked.

Norma will deal with the Hunter $$

Two names that meant nothing to her.

Yet, Amelia was elated. The entry raised more questions than it answered, but she knew it had to be important because it was written in code.

But why would Corey meticulously incriminate himself in these journals only to write a single sentence in code?

Norma will deal with the Hunter $$. What could it mean? Was Corey referring to an accomplice, perhaps the man who had taken Daisy as the "Hunter?" And who was Norma?

Amelia stared at the entry until her eyes burned. It wasn't until 5 am that she noticed the 'H' in Hunter was capitalised. Was it a name...or a nickname?

The only person she had ever heard of who was actually christened Hunter was Hunter S Thompson. He was the founder of Gonzo Journalism, a form of journalism that supposedly shunned objectivity. Was it possible Corey was referring to Herb, the gutter-dwelling paparazzo? He could certainly be described as lacking in objectivity.

Why would he give Herb a codename? And how does this help me, seeing as Herb is dead?

Just think about it, Inner-Maud said. *Daisy would have recognised him if he'd been involved in the kidnapping, so those dollar signs can only mean one thing.*

'Blackmail!' Amelia shouted, startling the dogs, who leapt to their feet, ready for action. She let out a deep breath. 'Calm down, my loves. I've just had a eureka moment.'

So, Herb had known more about the kidnapping than he ever told, because he was blackmailing Corey and this Norma. But who is Norma? Is it a person or another codename? Maybe Herb's paparazzi pad will hold some clues, she thought, rifling through the journals and papers until she found it.

Amelia almost screamed in frustration when she realised the pad was filled with shorthand notes. Every page was covered in loops and swirls that meant nothing to her. She flicked through the pages and realised that all the names and places were written out in full. She went back to the beginning, looking for names, and about halfway through the pad she found it.

Norma.

It might not be much—she couldn't understand the squiggles around the name—but it still held a clue. *The pad isn't fifteen years old like Corey's journals. It's the pad Herb was using on this trip, which means Norma is here on the island,* Amelia thought, laying the pad down beside her on the bed as she yawned.

It was time for sleep. She was running on empty. *No, I have to keep going. It's the only way I can save Daisy...and my inheritance.*

But the weight of the day took its toll, and only seconds later, she zonked out on the bed, notes and symbols and clues surrounding her as she dreamt of the shadow artist furiously painting Daisy in ominous shades of black and white.

CHAPTER TWELVE

Amelia dragged her sleep deprived body down to the dining room in an even sorrier state than she had the previous morning. Yesterday had begun with tired optimism, while today was more jaded hopelessness. But she had that clue to hang onto—a code name—which was more than she'd had the night before.

It was Saturday, only twelve hours before a hundred guests were due to arrive on the island; an island where a murderer was on the loose. The depressing question that revolved around her mind, over and over, was: *Can I figure out the identity of that murderer—and catch them—before 9 pm, or will I be turning my guests away at the dock?*

If she turned them away, she'd lose everything. All her hard work for naught. Her future, uncertain; her life a shambles.

But I refuse to endanger anyone else for my own selfish ends.

She shuffled to the buffet and filled a cup of coffee. Then, instead of jumping into breakfast preparations, she stood staring at the dining table where, the previous morning, Oliver swept the space between Herb's and Daisy's places. There had been a little pile of dried seaweed brought in from the beach.

She spat a stream of coffee back into her cup.

Where did the seaweed come from?

Not from Daisy; she'd been wearing a gorgeous pair of Louboutin red-soled shoes. Amelia would have noticed the sacrilege if those had been covered with seaweed. So, that meant Herb dragged it in. But from where?

He'd admitted to going exploring, but in their preparations, David and Pau had used the decrepit old tractor to clear the beach of any unsightly blemishes to its golden perfection. Most of the coastline was made up of rocky outcrops and cliffs too high for seaweed to reach, which only left the harbour. Herb had to have gone there some time before dinner.

But what does it matter, damn it! That was hours before David's murder and Herb is dead. He didn't kill himself! Inner-Maud scolded.

Give me a minute! Amelia snapped. *Something about that seaweed is important. I know it!*

'Oh, there you are,' Leo called, striding into the room looking disgustingly handsome and unreasonably refreshed while her stomach felt like the inside of a food mixer.

'Did you know the entirety of the island population, bar the goats, slept in your drawing room?' he asked.

'Don't be ridiculous, Leo. Maud would never deign—'

'Don't believe me? Just come and take a peek,' he said tiptoeing across to the connecting door.

Halfway across the room, Amelia realised she too was tiptoeing. She giggled. Then, remembering two people were dead, she schooled her face. Leo had a talent for making her laugh, even at the very worst moments of her life.

Peeping around the door, she saw Maud and Wendy like bookends at either end of the sofa, Price curled up like a sleeping child in the loveseat by the window. Violet, Pau, Barron, and the shadow artist were slouched in big armchairs. Sawubona and Tantriana sat meditating, crossed legged, although Amelia thought she might have heard snoring coming from their direction. The whole group made an oddly endearing sight that had Amelia smiling as she turned away.

'They're spooked.'

'They're being quite ridiculous,' she replied, fighting a smile.

Leo grinned unrepentantly, then said, 'Oliver is seeing to Daisy, who he has locked in her room. Good thing you had all those window locks and such installed.'

'*Leo!*' she hissed, her smile vanishing. 'This is no joking matter.'

'I know, old duck. I can't help cracking stupid jokes when I'm nervous,' he said with an apologetic smile. 'Let's start again. Good morning, Amelia. What's on the sleuthing agenda today?'

'Are you up for a tour of the island?' she asked.

'A tour? Will you give me a clue as to where before I commit?'

'First, to the marina. I want to search David's yacht again. I couldn't face it before, but there must be something I missed in my first search.'

Leo held up one hand as he poured himself a coffee and stirred it absently as she talked.

'After that, I want to have another look around both Herb's murder scene and the artists' community.'

'Shall we take a picnic?'

'No, no picnic. Not with two murder scenes on the agenda.'

'This is where I found the passports and the money,' Amelia said, opening the now empty fridge. Oliver hadn't exactly cleaned up—that would be tampering with evidence. But he had righted the upturned furniture and thrown a blanket over the stained floor. The smell had faded as the blood dried, but a wave of revulsion flowed through Amelia as she imagined tiny particles of David floating around in the air like dust motes. She instantly regretted conjuring the image, tamping it down as she moved to studying the room.

'Look for little details. It doesn't matter how small or insignificant something might seem. If it tells us more about David and what he was doing here, then it's important. From your experience with the man, as well as Wendy's and Daisy's, his chequered past will be our best clue to who had motive to kill him,' Amelia said.

'Everyone he ever met, I'd say,' Leo muttered as he began searching through the kitchen cupboards.

She looked through the mess on the desk, where Oliver or Pau had piled the mess from the floor. There was the lamp, some fishing lures, the two storage boxes of stationery, and the *Barco-lona* magazine she had last seen face down in a pool of blood which was now dried, sticking the pages together.

After rooting through the boxes of stationery, she noticed a detail about the magazine that she couldn't have seen the day of the murder. It had been face-down, but now it was face up and open on the centre spread. The photographer's visit had been months ago, but she couldn't fail to recognise her own island.

The main photo was a wide-angled shot of the hotel art gallery, its walls festooned with paintings. Beside it were several more photographs of individual paintings and mosaics. Finally, there was a photograph of Amelia and the artists standing in front of the cabins. It was an article that had put the El Pedrusco artists' community on the map. *How odd. I can't imagine where David found that old thing.*

As she wandered over to David's tools, Amelia noticed that his captain's hat was still hanging amongst his outdoor gear. It was the exact same design as the one she'd found by Herb's body the night before.

Now that her head was clearer, she realised the tools were in exactly the same position they had been in when she had delivered him a late supper two nights before his murder. Come to think of it, she'd never seen them move from their current position the entire month David had been marooned there. Knowing what she now knew about his character, she now doubted a broken-down boat was the real reason for his arrival at El Pedrusco.

Once again, she was faced with more questions than answers. She sighed and went back to searching.

They must have been through every drawer, cupboard, and cubbyhole on the yacht. *Even in death, David is keeping his secrets,* Amelia thought as she prepared to leave.

As she climbed up onto the deck, she wondered what would happen to the *Titanic* now. Its captain was dead so it needed a new one, but who would inherit it? Did David have any family? Could a monster like him have a family? *Of course, monsters have families,* she chided herself.

These were her thoughts as they took the mountain path, heading to the second murder scene. The path was far more beaten down than it had been before her guests arrived.

'Do you remember that year when we were all here?' she asked, and Leo's gaze swung to meet hers. 'We'd only met a few months earlier; I was seven and you were nine. Uncle Seb invited you and Bennet here for the summer.'

Leo nodded and smiled. 'Mum had been gone two years by then, and Dad never did know what to do during the summer break.'

'Yup. Oliver and Uncle Seb put up some old army tents in the clearing where the artists' community is now, and Oliver spent the whole summer teaching us how to survive if we were ever stranded in the wilderness.'

'Do you remember when your dad would creep out of the big house late at night to bring us chocolate and tell us spooky stories until we begged him to stop?' Leo laughed at the memory. Amelia nodded, smiling despite herself. *If only we could go back to those times.*

They'd reached the second scene by then, and continued to chat while they searched around the base of the olive tree and the clearing, before moving into the brush.

'That summer really was grand, wasn't it? The only summer we had everyone together before Maynard and Bennet disappeared,' Leo said, his voice tinged with sadness. Then his face brightened, a smile sweeping across it. 'But it wasn't as grand as the year Seb tried to teach us to sail. You spent more time with your head over the side of the boat than you did listening to his instructions,' Leo teased.

Amelia was ready to give up their search and move on. She moved back towards the path as she commented, 'You were quite the little sailor after that summer. Have you kept it up?'

'I have,' Leo said, then hesitated before adding, 'Seb and I spent a week aboard *As You Like It* every year for the last seven,' he admitted, watching her with a guarded expression.

Amelia changed the subject, though her expression might have given away her shock. Uncle Seb had never shared that little morsel. 'Can't find anything. Shall we continue our tour?' she asked.

Five minutes later, they stopped for a drink of water. Amelia settled herself on a rocky outcrop that overlooked the lake so they could enjoy watching the flamingos wade in the shallow depths below. Some of the older ones were pure pink, but others were half white, with patches of pink on their wings. Amelia smiled, remembering the beauty of them flocking that first night.

Is it ghoulish to hope Herb's photograph comes out?

His camera lens had been broken in the struggle, but the film compartment hadn't popped open. There was a chance the film could be saved, and it was a good thing too—that was a once-in-a-lifetime shot.

Amelia gasped.

'What is it?' Leo asked.

'Hang on. Let me think...' she said, holding her hand up to quiet him. 'Leo... What if David was murdered *before* dinner?' Leo just looked puzzled.

'Think about it! Herb was acting suspicious. He was late for dinner and there was seaweed under the table where he sat...'

She frowned, thinking about dinner, putting the pieces together. 'The flamingos flocked before dinner because they were startled...and the only place on this island you can get seaweed on your shoes is the marina. Herb had to have visited David's boat.'

'I don't understand, Lia. Are you saying Herb murdered David before dinner?' Leo asked. 'But didn't you see David at midnight? And, in case you forgot, Herb was *murdered*.'

'Think about it. If I hadn't seen David and that stranger down on the beach, what evidence would we have that he wasn't murdered earlier?' she asked.

'None?'

She knew she was onto something, but as Leo said, Herb had been murdered too, so she couldn't see how the flamingo revelation helped her.

Amelia sighed before screwing the lid back onto the water bottle so they could continue their strange tour. This time they were headed for the artists' community.

The community consisted of six cabins, three of which were occupied full time by the artists currently camped out in her drawing room. Uncle Seb had built the other three for artists now long since gone. That emptiness leant the community the echoing loneliness of one of those old, abandoned mining towns.

'It's a shame we can't have a look inside,' Leo mourned. 'We should have asked for permission to snoop before we left.'

'Oh, don't be silly. Nobody's going to mind if we just pop our heads around the door,' Amelia replied, infusing her words with as much confidence as she could muster. Leo didn't look convinced, but his shrug indicated capitulation.

This had been Amelia's plan as soon as she saw them sleeping like babes back at the hotel. Her mind had instantly jumped to the idea of having a good snoop without anyone looking over her shoulder.

What did that say about her? Poor Leo would be shocked at her deceit.

'You check Violet's cabin while I look in Barron's,' she ordered. 'We can both search the shadow artist's cabin before we head back.'

When she stepped inside Barron's cabin, she was shocked. It smelled like a bordello, the scents of Paco Rabanne and patchouli oil warring for dominance. What's more, it looked like a hurricane had swept through it. There were items of clothing from his fancy dress boxes strewn all over the place: a red, velvet smoking jacket, two dinner jackets, an old-fashioned frock coat, and a navy tunic.

There were even a few pieces of Violet's lingerie lying on his bed alongside a pile of colourful canvasses. A notebook lay open on his desk. Amelia's heart raced. Maybe he was involved and she'd get lucky with a clue from his journal like she had with David's?

No. It was just a numbered list of paintings with detailed descriptions alongside.

The walls were lined with more canvasses, and there was an old-style women's bicycle with a wicker basket on the front leaning against one of the many, massive costume trunks.

I'd need a week to sort through all this! Amelia thought in horror before diving into her search. By the time she finished, she had turned up nothing to explain what had prompted Barron to come to the island. More importantly, there was nothing that pointed to him being the killer.

Disappointed, she walked over to Violet's cabin where she found Leo lying on his back, half under the bed, rummaging through storage boxes.

'Anything?' she asked.

'Not really,' he said, reversing himself out from under the bed. 'There are boxes and boxes of clothing and makeup, like she hoarded it all from old theatre and film productions.

'Oh, and it looks like she was telling the truth about firing those pots. There's a bunch over there that look ready to glaze.'

There was a modern kiln and some first-fired pots set out on a table. Amelia noticed a huge multi-coloured mosaic vase in one corner; it looked valuable, but Violet was using it as an umbrella stand. Nothing unexpected or suspicious.

'I couldn't find anything incriminating, I'm afraid,' Leo said, mirroring her thoughts.

'Alright, let's just check the shadow artist's cabin quick, then we can head back.'

The final cabin was dark. The windows were covered with black fabric to ward off the sun. *He's like a vampire,* Amelia thought with a shudder.

It was a barren place. The floor was unvarnished, the kitchen table and worksurfaces were bare, the wardrobe was half-empty, and the few items of clothing inside were mismatched and heavily worn.

It's as if he's only half alive, she thought as they went to work, turning out every drawer and checking every tube of paint.

Next, she moved onto the paintings. Many were hung on the walls or stood on easels. Still more were leaning, three deep, along the perimeter of the walls.

All were monochrome, like the gloom of a grey London day. They were filled with melancholy, as if every brushstroke was an expression of his yearning for a light he could never fully experience. But Amelia had to admit they were powerful too, quite moving.

On the far side of his bed, Amelia spotted the painting from the day before on an easel; the one that showed Daisy creeping around in the darkness. Standing beside it, on another easel, was its twin.

Its non-identical twin.

The tones of the second painting were a touch lighter, as if it had been painted earlier, at dusk. The artist had used paler hues for the sky, the trees, and bushes, to mimic the last rays of the sun.

There was another difference too; one that was damning. Amelia's heart sank.

The woman carried a captain's hat, just like the one Chessie found near Herb's body.

Amelia tilted her head, considered the angle of the second painting, then crossed to the rear of the cabin to pull back the fabric from the heavily draped window. *It could have been painted from here, looking up at the path Leo and I just came down.*

'Shit!' Leo gasped from beside her, noticing the second painting. 'It's Daisy. She really did it.'

Amelia had to agree. On the face of it, the painting did appear to implicate Daisy.

But it was the thing that *wasn't* different in the second painting that caught Amelia's eye. The very thing that seemed to point to Daisy provided Amelia with the final piece of the jigsaw.

She had everything she needed to unmask the murderer, but as she swung open the door, allowing light to flow into the gloomy space, she spotted a splash of colour on one of the paintings. She froze.

How can this be?

The painting was old… *Twenty-two years old.*

It was a guess, of course, but she knew she couldn't be far wrong because the man in the painting looked exactly as he had the last time she had seen him.

'Should we go back?' Leo asked, his voice resigned as he came to stand beside her. 'Wow…isn't that—?'

Tears welled in her eyes. It wasn't a formal portrait. It was one of those slightly caricature-ish ones those seaside artists painted. The man in the foreground was standing on a palm-lined promenade. Amelia recognised it instantly as the *Promenade des Anglais* in Nice. Amelia had been there many times herself, when her uncle had taken her sailing in his yacht, *As You Like It*.

Dead centre, there was a man wearing sunglasses and a Panama hat, staring out over a packed beach. The painting was in colour.

'Yes,' she croaked, snatching the painting out of his reach. 'It's my father.'

'Where the devil—?'

'Come on,' she said, interrupting him, not ready for this discussion.

'But Lia, that's Nice, where *As You Like It* is moored... Do you think they're still—?'

'Stop!' Amelia snapped, not ready to think about Sebastian smuggling their fathers out of France, or what might have happened to cause him to do that. 'We need to deal with *this* problem before we move on to the *next*.'

Leo shot her an angry look that wasn't difficult to read. Leo had lost his mother to cancer and, only a couple of years later, he'd lost his father. *This isn't all about you Amelia,* Inner-Maud informed her haughtily. *This is Leo's mystery too.*

Amelia sighed. 'I'm sorry, Leo. We will talk about it, I promise. But for now, let's go back to the hotel. I have some thinking to do while you gather everyone—including Daisy and Oliver—together in the drawing room. I'll meet you there in an hour,' she said.

'It's time for our murderer to be unveiled.'

CHAPTER THIRTEEN

Amelia glanced at the clock as she crossed the grand reception hall, headed to the drawing room. One o'clock; the staff would be back in a couple of hours. Jordi would get busy putting together a feast fit for their esteemed guests while Estell and Mar went full Cinderella on the public areas. The party guests would sail into the harbour in style on the romantic Turkish gullet around four hours after that, which left Amelia six hours; not much time to unmask a murderer, set up for a grand gala, and transform herself into the proverbial Hostess-with-the-mostess.

As she walked through the stained-glass entrance on shaking legs, Amelia was met by a sea of expectant faces. They were all there, even Daisy, who was glassy eyed but placid. Oliver was perched on the arm of her chair, his hand resting on her shoulder, either to offer comfort, or to hold her back.

The room's normally bright and inviting atmosphere was heavily shrouded in deference to their shadow artist, though Amelia had little doubt that the dark events of the past days would have dulled its lustre anyway.

Amelia now knew which of her guests was a murderer, but she regretted the inevitable wounds the revelation would open.

She glanced around the room, her gaze pausing for a moment on Maud, whose problems she'd been solving since the moment she learned how to pour the perfect martini at the age of seven.

'Well?' Leo asked. She turned to him and smiled. At the beginning of this mystery—was it really only two days ago?—she had thought of Leo as someone her Uncle Seb had foisted on her, a necessary pawn in this game he seemed to be playing with her; a game for which she had not been provided with the rulebook.

Now, she could feel something more than history or a residual fondness growing in her heart for this strange, awkward man who stood stiff at the unlit fireplace, his left-hand wrapped around the mantle like he was gripping on for dear life. Shock at the events of the last few days was setting in, not just for him, but for them all.

Best get this over with.

'Thank you for joining me here,' she began. 'I know this has been a horrifying time for us all.'

'It has been intolerable,' Maud complained. 'I have been accused, berated, and forced to sleep in a chair. It is time for me to leave.'

'At last, a plan I can get onboard with,' Price agreed. 'I'll warrant, if I can get off this damned rock before nightfall, I might just persuade that studio exec to reschedule yesterday's meeting.'

'I thought I would never want to leave this island, but with some maniac running around this resort, murdering people,' Violet said, her eyes purposefully avoiding her daughter's, 'I'm afraid we would be foolhardy to remain.'

'I'm sorry,' Amelia said, shaking her head. 'The staff will be back in two hours. You can leave as soon as they arrive.' She would lose everything if Daisy and Leo did, but like Price said: could she really blame them for wanting off this rock?

'The selfish people think only of themselves,' Pau said. 'They do not care *for los muertos*. But Pau, he wants to know who has killed two people and stolen *las sonrisas* from our faces.'

'Well said, Farero,' Oliver said. 'Just get on with it and tell us who killed David and Herb.'

Amelia nodded and cleared her throat.

'Let's begin with the weirdness on the driveway on Thursday afternoon. David and Pau were arguing when we arrived. That wasn't particularly shocking—they'd been daggers drawn from the get-go. What was surprising was the way everyone froze when David came over to say hello.'

'After getting settled in your rooms and taking a siesta, Price went exploring, Oliver went back to his chores, and the rest of you went with me to the shrine room for a yoga class. While I was twisted in a knot, Violet arrived in her guise as Beatrice Besson, and it was then I noticed that Violet, Herb, and Daisy had left the room. Was it possible that one of them had recognised Violet?

'Then, while out on our sunset birdwatching foray, I noticed how oddly Daisy was acting, tottering along the cliffs in platform shoes, staring at David through her binoculars, then talking in riddles about the boogieman. I was desperately worried about her. Nothing bad had happened yet, but I still had a feeling that Daisy was heading for a fall.' Daisy, hollow-cheeked and visibly shaking, glanced briefly at Amelia, then ducked her head.

'Next came that spectacular flamingo murmuration, followed by dinner, where Wendy shared her ordeal back in London. Still, nothing seemed amiss, and soon after, we removed ourselves to the drawing room for drinks and a game of bridge.

'Once again, Daisy was behaving oddly. If we were actors in a film, I'd have complained of how heavy-handed the writing was, how obvious it was who the murderer was...and that was just the beginning—'

'It so strange,' Wendy interrupted. 'I remember commenting on it to Tantriana. Daisy only had two drinks all evening, but by the time she went to bed, she could barely walk.'

'That's right...and then Herb insisted on escorting her to bed,' Amelia added. 'The rest of us dispersed soon after. Oliver and I retired to the office to work on the next day's itinerary, after which I went down for a swim. That was when I spotted David on the beach talking to a stranger.'

Her guests had shifted forward in their seats. This was new information to many of them. Amelia began to pace as she continued her story.

'As I watched them argue, I'm ashamed to say I made an understandable, but incorrect, supposition about that scene on the beach. I had my swim then went to bed. Next morning, I went in search of David, only to find him murdered.'

'And I was with you. Such a terrible shock; I'm sure I'll never forget it!' Maud exclaimed.

'Yes, you were, Mother, and at that grisly crime scene, while raiding the fridge to find you water, I found literal piles of cash and those three passports, all of them David's but issued in different names. It seemed to me our victim had secrets that might point to his murderer. Then, after I sent Maud off to find Oliver, I found an ornate key on a chain around David's neck.'

Amelia pulled the key from her pocket and showed them. Daisy flinched.

'Oh yes, he kept trophies, little trinkets to remind himself of a little girl's suffering. It's despicable,' Amelia said, her voice harsh with anger.

'I learned soon after that many of you already knew David. Leo and Wendy had both met him in London, not as David Ash, but as Dominic Strathclere, and both had been terrorized in their own way.

'As for Maud, Violet, and Daisy,' she said, eyes scanning the three women,' you knew him fifteen years ago, under another guise—that of Corey Wilson—first as an aspiring actor, then as a suspected kidnapper.'

'An all-around bad actor who probably deserved what he got,' Price growled, his frown lines punctuated on his pudgy face.

Amelia could hardly disagree, but murder was murder. 'By late morning, I had pinned down the time of death to between 12.30 and 2.30 in the morning.'

'That's right,' Oliver said. 'You reasoned that if the dust from the rainstorm hadn't been disturbed on the deck of his yacht, he must have been murdered before the storm.'

Amelia nodded. 'At lunch, many of you provided me with indisputable alibis. Then there were the rest: Leo, Daisy, Price, Wendy, Herb, Pau, Barron, and our shadow artist. However, of those guests, only Daisy, Wendy and Leo appeared to have motive.' Amelia nodded to the three of them as she spoke their names, though she doubted the gesture softened the blow of her accusation.

'That day, Herb tagged along on my tour of the island, even as I made my way to the artists' community. I was hoping against hope that I'd find a suspect with a clear motive and opportunity who wasn't one of my esteemed guests. Instead, I found a painting of a slender woman in an evening gown creeping around in the undergrowth after dark. The shadow artist told me he painted it late Thursday night. Again, my best clue pointed at Daisy.'

'As I left the artists' community, I noticed Herb chatting with Violet, and as he bade her goodbye, he gave this strange little salute; the exact same salute the mystery person gave down on the beach the night before. If Herb was that person, I asked myself, had he followed David back to his yacht, murdered him and walked back to the hotel in time to complain about a missing bulb at his bungalow at 1.30 am?'

'Did he have time?' Wendy asked.

Amelia smirked. 'As I came to find out, the answer to that question doesn't matter. You see, I had been misled. The time of death I had landed on was all wrong, because when I came down to breakfast this morning, I remembered the *seaweed*.'

'Where are you going with this Lia?' Leo asked.

'Patience,' she said, winking at Leo before addressing the room once again. 'After I noticed Herb's odd salute, I went back to the hotel where I spoke to Maud, who pointed a finger firmly at you Leo, then

I spoke to Daisy who managed to implicate herself still further by exposing David as her kidnapper.

'After that, I had every intention of finding Herb and confronting him about being on the beach with David late on Thursday evening. I brought Leo along with me.'

'As a bodyguard, of course,' he added.

'I remember it quite differently,' Amelia said, repressing a laugh. 'We took our walk, we chatted, and when I confronted you about your dealings with David, you inadvertently gave me another little clue when you told me about that mysterious conversation you overheard.' She turned to her mother. 'About how Maud had denied being at fault. *"How could I have known the toy boy would show up?"*' Amelia imitated her mother. 'Which was odd because I had never known my mother to have had a toy boy. How could she when she barely left the house?'

'Then, on the way back to the hotel, we discovered Herb's body. Your prime suspect was dead...' Leo said.

Amelia was quiet, reliving the discovery before continuing. 'I found clues at the scene: a piece of fabric and a captain's hat.

'After that, things moved rapidly. Daisy disappeared, the artists arrived, and Beatrice revealed herself as Violet. As the evidence mounted, everyone settled into the idea of Daisy being a murderer. Even you,' she said, her accusing eyes moving first to Oliver and then Price.

Price harrumphed at that, slammed his glass down near the decanter, and poured himself a straight whiskey. 'Ridiculous! Completely ridiculous!'

'Pour me one,' Oliver said. He was sweating through his Aertex uniform shirt. Amelia had never seen him so frazzled as Price splashed whiskey into another glass. 'Amelia, dear, even with everything you've presented, it does seem awfully open and shut. How can it not be Daisy?'

'That *is* the question, isn't it?' Amelia replied. 'Leo and I searched and searched for Daisy, and after hours of searching, we found her in Herb's room. She wasn't in her right mind,' she said, looking at Daisy. 'Nor should you have been. You had read every page of Corey's terrible journals and had been triggered into a post-traumatic fugue state.'

'Did you read them?' Daisy asked, surprising everyone in the room.

'I did... I read them, and I still can't quite believe—'

'Norma will deal with the Hunter $$,' Daisy whispered, eyes brimming with tears.

'Hold your horses,' Price demanded, holding his hands in the air, his quick mind chewing on Amelia's words. 'How 'bout we just back up for a moment and you tell us about the damned seaweed.'

'Oh that... Well, that's just what I was getting to. I read the journals then dragged myself down to breakfast where I remembered the seaweed, then later, on the way to Herb's murder scene, I thought about the flamingos,' she explained.

'The seaweed,' Oliver repeated, scratching his head. 'Under the table?'

'Yes. On Friday morning, when I came down to breakfast, you were cleaning seaweed from under the table. Seaweed that could only have got there at dinner the night before. It was between Herb's and Daisy's places.'

'It can't have been mine,' Daisy said, finding more courage. She stood a little straighter. 'I had on my Louboutin's. I've never even worn them outdoors, let alone stomped around in the sea. They're far too precious.'

Amelia was relieved that Daisy still had some life in her. 'Yes, I did notice your shoes, Daisy. Herb, on the other hand, arrived at dinner far later than everyone else, having been delayed photographing the flamingos, and by that time, deep in conversation, I was beyond noticing the condition of his shoes.'

'What are you *talking* about,' Price asked, boring a hole into Amelia. 'You damned English never get to the point of it. Who the hell is it!'

'Be quiet, Peppy,' Daisy ordered. 'Have some patience and let her explain.'

'Thank you,' Amelia said, then heaved in a deep breath, before continuing. 'Last week, Pau and David cleaned the seaweed from the beach in honour of your arrival. It is a time consuming and laborious task.' Pau grunted in agreement.

'The thing is, other than the beach and the marina, the entire coastline is made up of high cliffs and rocky outcrops.'

'And?' Price asked.

'Don't you see? With the beach thoroughly cleaned, Herb could only have collected that seaweed at the marina. And there is only one reason I can think of for him to have walked for thirty minutes back to that marina...'

'To visit David,' Sawubona said with quiet confidence. 'He was murdered before dinner, not after.'

There was a flutter of gasps and murmurs. They all looked at Amelia, and she nodded, confirming Sawubona's surprising conclusion. Until now, it seemed as if he and Tantriana were barely listening.

'That means nothing. Herb might have gone to the marina for any number of reasons,' Violet objected.

'You're right, Violet. It proves nothing,' Amelia replied.

'Maybe the flamingos explain the rest?' Leo suggested.

'To explain the flamingos, I need to take you back to this morning, after I remembered the seaweed.

'Everyone was asleep in the drawing room, so I decided to take the opportunity to go to the murder scenes and the artists' community. It would likely be my last chance to search without anyone looking over my shoulder.'

'We went to the *Titanic* first,' Leo said. 'Nothing much to see there.'

'Or was there?' Price guessed, watching Amelia's reaction.

'Perhaps,' she agreed. 'Though one item confirmed something I already knew, and another sparked a new line of thinking.'

'What's that?' Price asked.

'Amongst David's possessions I found a copy of a *Barco-lona* magazine. It contained a centre spread on the island and the artists and featured an interview I gave about the new hotel and the opening party.'

'What does that prove?' Violet asked. 'You courted that publicity yourself.'

'Indeed, but I know for a fact that David did not find that magazine in the hotel. I was only ever sent one copy for my files, and that copy is still in the cabinet where I left it. I mention it because it adds credence to my theory that David came here for other reasons.

'My best guess is he picked up a copy of the magazine when he was buying his yacht. Perhaps he recognised me, or the name of one of the famous guests due to attend the gala, or perhaps even one of our permanent residents. Whatever or whomever he recognised, it's not much of a leap to surmise that the magazine gave him an idea for his next racket. And the unused tools I found lined up neatly in his yacht were merely props for his little Robinson Crusoe charade.'

'*Sí*. I worked with him many times this month, always on the preparations for your *fiesta*. Never once does he ask me for help with the boat,' Pau said. Then he chuckled before adding. 'In case you wonder why I did not offer help. It is because I did not like him.'

'There was something else?' Violet asked, unmoved by Pau's light-heartedness.

'David's captain's hat,' Amelia said. She walked over to her bag, pulled the hat out of it, and tossed it across the room. It landed on the coffee table, right next to the captain's hat Chessie found near the scene of Herb's murder. Identical twins.

'There are two?' Price asked, shooting back his glass of whiskey. He was sweating profusely. 'What does that tell us?'

'I think it confirms that David was not the person I saw arguing with Herb at midnight,' Amelia replied.

'I believe one of those hats might be mine.' Barron was seated on a highbacked antique chair, legs crossed at the ankle, wearing a black, velvet frock coat with silver buttons. 'I have one just like it. It is part of my sailor costume, but I have not seen it recently.'

Amelia wasn't surprised.

'Next, Leo and I left David's yacht and walked around the lake to the site of Herb's murder, where I had found the initial captain's hat. Afterwards, we stopped for some water and to watch the flamingos, which was the moment I put together all these small clues and realised how wrong I had been about everything.'

'Ah-ha! I wondered when you would get to the flamingos,' Price exclaimed, rolling his eyes.

Amelia huffed. 'As we rested up and watched the birds, I remembered something Oliver had once said about them flocking. He had never seen the flamingos behave like that. They wade about and eat. They have no sense of drama, and they definitely don't go out of their way to provide spectacles grand enough to be on the cover of the *National Geographic*. No...my flamingos were scared by the sound of a gunshot.'

'Gunshot? You mean...' Wendy muttered, trailing off.

Amelia nodded. 'Yes, but first let me tell you about the rest of my tour.'

'What? No! Explain the damned flamingos!' Price exploded, but Amelia shook her head.

'I'm ashamed to say we took advantage of everyone being here at the hotel, and snooped in all the artists' cabins,' she said to the artists. 'It was my idea. Leo was against it from the outset.'

'This invasion is intolerable! Your uncle might have left you this island, but he left my cabin to me outright!' Barron exploded, his words the most passionate she had ever heard from him. With his outlandish fancy dress, and the way he screwed up his face in anger, Amelia half expected him to stamp his foot. She sighed.

'Never mind their bloody privacy. Did you find anything?' Maud asked, impatient, her foot tapping like a metronome on the tiled floor.

'Oh yes. We found something alright,' Amelia replied. 'We found trunks full of clothes in Barron's cabin, all of which would make for a good disguise. There was nothing in Violet's cabin, but when we searched the shadow artist's cabin, we struck gold,' Amelia revealed, while Leo nodded glumly. It was clear he still thought Daisy was guilty.

To her surprise, the shadow artist did not flinch at her words. He remained huddled in the corner, fingers laced together, eyes pointed at the floor near Amelia's feet.

'Not only did we find the now completed painting I had spotted on my first visit—a painting of a willowy woman creeping through the darkness, with pale hair and a long dress—but on the easel right next to it was a second matching painting. This one was brighter somehow, as if it had been painted earlier in the day. The subject looked to be the same woman, this time walking down the path above the artists' village. She was wearing an evening dress and carrying a captain's hat. As I stood, gazing at the different light of the two paintings, misery tapping on my shoulder, I saw what the artist saw, and all the clues fell into place.'

Amelia watched as Leo looked at Daisy uneasily. It set her off.

'That doesn't prove anything! Everyone knows my dress for tomorrow's party was stolen!' Daisy exclaimed, tears flowing like twin rivers down her face.

'The clues all added up: a missing dress, untouched tools, the flight of the flamingos, two shadow paintings, two captain's hats, a magazine, cryptic journals, and seaweed under the table,' Amelia said.

'For goodness sakes, will you—' Maud snapped.

'Mother, *shut up,*' Amelia said, staring daggers at Maud. The old drama queen nearly fell over from shock. She wasn't about to let her steal this from her. *Not this time.* 'As soon as David's past was revealed, I tried to consider our killer's motive. I looked at the problem as I would if I was casting a play. Who seemed to have the best alibi and who would be the most convincing in the role of murderer? In all my endeavours, I could see only five cast members who gave off the *feel* of a murderer and who also had motive to kill David.

'There was Wendy, who was stalked mercilessly, Leo whose good name had been ruined, and Daisy who was kidnapped and tormented. Those three were clear, but we can't forget Violet, Daisy's distraught mother, perhaps looking for vengeance against her daughter's kidnapper...and my own mother, Maud.'

'What!' Maud squeaked, recovering from her earlier shock. '*Me?!*'

'Why Maud?' Leo asked.

'Shame and guilt, of course. Daisy let slip to me that Maud was meant to collect her from her ballet class on the day she was taken. Imagine the guilt she must have lived with all these years.'

'The toy boy,' Price murmured.

'Yes,' Amelia agreed. 'Leo overheard a conversation between Violet and Maud, in which Maud insisted that she could not have known the toy boy would turn up. Do you see? Maud, contrary to what she told Violet—and I know from experience that she regularly makes statements contrary to what she in fact believes—does blame herself for Daisy's kidnapping, and what's more, her insistence that she couldn't have known leads me to believe that she, like Violet, knew that Corey was involved.'

'I did not!' Maud screeched.

'*Mother*,' Amelia warned, and to her surprise, Maud piped down. 'We have five contenders for the role of murderer, all of them playing their parts to perfection. So, which of them had alibis for David's murder if it took place before the flight of the flamingos at 8 pm, and not midnight?

'I know they say that eavesdroppers never hear good of themselves, but in this case Leo's eavesdropping before dinner not only provided him with an alibi but inadvertently gave one to Maud and Violet too. Three down, two to go; Wendy and Daisy.'

'I was in my room when I heard the gong. I was hungry...and a little lonely...so I hurried downstairs. I am sure I reached the dining room for a quarter past eight,' Wendy explained.

'It was twenty past—but yes, still not enough time to murder David at eight o'clock and make it back to the hotel. Which leaves Daisy, who arrived at around half past the hour. I have walked that rocky three-kilometre path to David's boat countless times and never once has that walk taken anything less than forty minutes. The police, or perhaps a gazelle, might prove me wrong, but it is my honest belief that Daisy could not have murdered David.'

'Which brings us back to Herb, dammit,' Price growled, pulling Daisy closer to him in a stiff hug.

'Price is right,' Amelia said. 'Every scrap of evidence points to Herb as being our murderer, though I am willing to concede it could easily have been an accident.'

'Accident or not, Herb is dead, murdered in cold blood by someone right here in this room,' Wendy said, her eyes scanning the room. 'This isn't solved, Amelia.'

CHAPTER FOURTEEN

Wendy was right, of course. What had been revealed had only been a part of the story. What came next would be bittersweet.

'Last night, after Leo and I found Daisy, I went to my suite determined to read every word in those journals. I was certain they must hold some clue to David's murder. Every page, every word, was excruciating. David, or Corey as we now know him, had not held back on the details...apart from that odd code written just days before Daisy's kidnapping: *"Norma will deal with the Hunter $$."'*

'What does it mean?' Leo asked.

'Hunter S Thompson was a journalist, so my guess is that Hunter was Corey's codename for Herb, and the dollar signs signified a payoff.'

'But why the hell would he need a codename?' Price asked.

'My thoughts exactly. He would only need one if he was part of Corey's little kidnap conspiracy.'

'That is simply ridiculous,' Maud said. Amelia ignored her. It was becoming exceedingly easier as the night wore on.

'I have pondered on how it might have happened. Perhaps, when we were taking sundowners on the summit of La Colina Alta, Herb spotted David through his telephoto lens, sitting on the deck of his yacht, recognised him as Corey-the-kidnapper, and took the first opportunity he had to hurry over there and confront him.

'After he returned to the hotel in the Land Cruiser, I imagine him sneaking off, taking the path to the marina, where the two men argued violently; a quarrel that ended with David lying dead on the floor, shot by his own gun. Unnerved, perhaps in shock, Herb hurried back to the hotel, stopping only to photograph flamingos, using their uncharacteristic dramatics, that he himself had caused, as an excuse for his lateness. It was actually quite shrewd. But when he told us the sky had turned pink, I realised he hadn't witnessed the display from the same angle as we had. For anyone at the hotel, the sky turned dark. For Herb, it turned pink. My guess is, when we develop that film, we'll see that Herb photographed those flamingos from close to the marina.'

'But why?' Wendy asked, her good heart blinding herself to human nature.

'Oh, that's simple. If he was involved in the kidnapping, or even if he was just paid off when he discovered the truth, he was most likely angling for another payday. Or maybe David turned the tables on him and threatened to implicate Herb and ruin his high-profile career in Hollywood? Either way, David was murdered by Herb Hogan...may he rest in peace.'

She looked around to gauge reactions; mostly shock, some guilt, and on Daisy's face...*defeat.*

'That was when Herb turned to his accomplice,' Amelia said after a bout of silence.

'Accomplice?' Oliver asked.

'Norma!' Price nearly yelled.

Clever man. Obnoxious, but clever.

Amelia nodded. 'Herb was our only murderer...until he himself was murdered. It stands to reason he was killed by an accomplice.'

Oliver said, 'So, David was murdered before dinner, and we know this because of the seaweed and the flamingos.'

'That's right,' Amelia replied. 'But before I tell you who our other coldblooded murderer is, let us consider the suspects, their alibis, and the evidence against them.'

'But surely this changes everything, doesn't it?' Leo said, befuddled as he ran a whole new plotline through his mind. 'We're no longer looking for someone who wanted David *and* Herb dead. Just the journalist!'

Amelia nodded. It had taken her a while to pivot to that new line of thinking too.

'Let's start with you, shall we Oliver? My uncle's companion and confidante, I have loved you for as long as I can remember,' she said. 'But I think we can all agree that your one great flaw, other than your horrible temperament, is your overblown sense of loyalty.' Oliver shrugged, unwilling to be drawn.

'My Uncle Seb undoubtedly shared with you everything he knew about Violet and Daisy and the kidnapping. Yet, you said nothing.' She turned to glare at her friend. '*Nothing*,' she repeated. Oliver glared unrepentantly back at her, silently defending his actions. *Loyalty above everything,* he seemed to say.

Amelia's own eyes were silently accusing, *Loyalty to the dead above the living?* Of course, Amelia was the first to break eye contact, though she did it with a very Maud-like *harrumph* and a dagger stare that said, *I have a killer to unmask, and you aren't helping me get that done.*

She turned away from Oliver to continue, 'Though, the fact he was busy with Pau, tinkering on the tractor, does give him something of a watertight alibi for Herb's murder. And that same alibi lets Pau and lucky old Price-is-right Peppy off the hook too, since our two worker-bees have grudgingly admitted to seeing him sunbathing on the beach.' Amelia noticed Price and Pau visibly relax at her words.

'And you, Leo, my darling? Lucky for you, you were walking at my side when Herb was killed, as we carried empty pails down from feeding the goats on La Colina Alta. So, my dearest Leo, you are in the clear,' Amelia said, giving her friend a small smile.

Amelia's eyes moved to her next suspect, their resident guru and his muse. 'I have learned a little about Sawubona and Tantriana having lived alongside them for almost a year. I have learned that they are far from your run-of-the-mill spiritual types, particularly when they're using my island as their own personal playground, but I can't for the life of me see any reason for either of them to team up with Herb to murder David,' she said.

'And even if they did have motive, when Leo and I caught sight of them on our way to that crime scene, they were skinny dipping in a spot too far from the scene for me to consider them suspects.' Sawubona grinned and Tantriana shot her a shy smile, as Amelia's thoughts moved to Hank.

'And our shadow artist was trapped in his hut at the time of Herb's murder, and of course, he was painting the second painting soon after. I am quite content neither man had the motive or opportunity.'

Next, she turned to Maud, but her mother's greatest secret had already been revealed—a secret she had taken great care to bury long ago under alcohol and bitterness. She was standing by the silver tray of crystal decanters, pouring out a scotch so large she may as well have been drinking directly from the bottle.

'And you, mother dearest, you could be the mysterious Norma in the journals. Intentionally "forgetting" to collect Daisy from her dance class on the day she was kidnapped could have been your part in the plot.'

'Intentionally?' Maud gasped, saturating that one word with decades of guilt. 'It wasn't my fault! I had been drinking... I fell asleep. I can hardly look at myself in the mirror for that small part I played, and you accuse me—!' her voice hitched as she collapsed into a chair and sobbed.

Amelia's soft heart almost tripped her up, but she couldn't show favouritism. Everyone had to go under the microscope, even Maud. 'Did the guilt eat you up until it turned into rage at the kidnappers? You recognised David on the driveway, didn't you? Is that why you conspired with your old friend Violet to provide each other an alibi?'

'Conspired,' Maud said. She elongated the syllables, like icicles stretching down from a roof.

'Tell me the truth. Did you really get lost on the path late at night?' Amelia asked, point blank. Maud hesitated, elongated her spine, and stiffened her neck, then shook her head once—no—but did not speak.

'When we were out on the terrace at lunch, you and I both spotted Violet—or Beatrice as she was then—coming out of the shrine room, didn't we?

You had no alibi for the night before, so relying on your long years of friendship, you raised your voice just enough to catch Violet's attention.

'After that, you spun your tale—getting lost on the path, coming across a lovely artist lady, yada-yada-yada—while, hidden from view, Violet listened, memorising every word. Which is how, when I visited the artists later, she was able to parrot back your entire story... *You*, with your secrets and lies!'

Having bludgeoned her with truth, Amelia offered her mother an olive branch. 'Though you lost my respect many years ago, and though I believe you fully capable of murdering someone, I cannot believe you would intentionally implicate your goddaughter after she had suffered so terribly.

'There is enough good left in you to keep you from heaping more pain on poor Daisy's shoulders.' Maud's own shoulders sagged in relief. 'And anyway, the lovely Wendy, who should hate you but apparently is far more forgiving than you deserve, has given you an alibi for the time of Herb's murder,' Amelia admitted, before turning to Daisy.

'Then there is Daisy, the person whom, after all is revealed, many would consider the real victim in all this. Whom, as we can all see, sits huddled like the child she was when these events were set in motion all those years ago. Back then, she and I were the very best of friends... I miss that,' Amelia said. Daisy raised her head just long enough to catch Amelia's eyes for a brief moment.

'You have been everyone's prime suspect ever since David's true identity as Corey-the-kidnapper was revealed. And I must say you have not helped yourself with your dramatic clifftop promenades and your dependence on prescription medication to keep the nightmares at bay. Though I would have denied it to my dying breath, you were my prime suspect too.' Daisy's shoulders slumped.

'Our shadow artist painted you wandering the island late on Thursday night. Daisy I need to know now: where were you going?'

'It was...I thought...' Daisy stumbled over her words.

'What did you think, Daisy?'

'I thought I was going mad when we got out of the car...and saw this David of yours. It dragged me back to a past I could never quite free myself from.' Daisy's tears were falling faster than she could swipe them away. She dragged in a fortifying breath, then continued, 'I spotted him again on the deck of that yacht. Smiling and waving, while I could barely keep my balance. Somehow, my nightmares were taking form...coming to life.'

'So, you went looking for him?' Oliver asked.

'Yes... I know what people think about me...but I hardly ever touch even a drop of alcohol. When you take ten pills a day just to keep the ghosts at bay, one glass of wine at dinner followed by the Irish coffee Herb forced on me had me staggering on my heels,' she explained, then hurried to say, 'Not that I blame anyone for what they thought.'

'What happened?' Price asked, worried.

'Herb was determined to escort me upstairs and, drunk and woozy as I was, it wasn't hard to pretend to be semi-conscious. I thought he'd put me to bed and leave, but instead, he riffled around in my belongings, while I lay there with one eye open, watching. Eventually he left, but not before he stole my party dress, which is one of a kind but...' She shrugged. 'It all seemed so strange and unnecessary. But he is a paparazzo, and I'm honestly used to this kind of...*attention*. I've found it much easier over the years to ignore it.'

'What then?' Amelia prompted.

'When he left my room I waited for a few minutes, mustering my courage, before sneaking out of my room and heading down the back stairs.'

'To the cliffs?' Maud asked.

'That nonsense is entirely your own invention, Mother.'

Amelia noticed Oliver had slid down from the arm into the chair beside Daisy, keeping his hand on her shoulder so that somehow his arm ended up around her. Daisy froze but did not shake him off. 'I've been scared of the boogieman my whole life and suddenly there he was. Perhaps it was Dutch courage from the alcohol that had me creeping down the stairs, or maybe I'd just had enough of being afraid. But I walked the mountain path, turning all possible scenarios over in my head. What I would say, what he would reply... Did I plan on killing him? I can't say the thought didn't cross my mind, but when I reached the boat…'

'What time was that?' Leo asked.

'It must have been around 1 am when I got there, and as you rightly surmised, he was already dead. It was horrible, but not undeserved.'

'What did you do?' Price asked, the first drop of shock showing on his face.

'I hurried back to the hotel, feeling…*lighter*.'

'Relief,' Wendy said in her quiet way.

Daisy nodded. 'I knew everything would come out and that I would be accused. I can't deny having the motive to murder that man,' Daisy said. 'But I did not kill him.'

'And Herb?' Oliver asked gently. 'Did you kill him?'

Daisy's eyes lit with the fire of indignation. It looked good on her. 'I had no reason to kill Herb,' she said. 'Although, later, after I had read Corey's journals, if he had still been alive then…'

'Daisy, I know you are not our murderer,' Amelia said.

'But how?' Leo asked.

'First, I believe it's prudent to ask who would *want* to disguise the time of the murder and why? For, as soon as I realised the time of death had been hidden on purpose, I knew it couldn't be her.'

'It couldn't?' Price asked, hopeful.

Amelia shook her head as she turned to stare out of the window. The warmth of the sun did nothing to cheer her. Now was the moment of truth. Her heart pounded and her voice shook as she spoke.

'Which brings us to you,' Amelia said, eyes boring into Violet's.

'So, it is my turn, is it?' Violet asked. 'My turn to have my character assassinated.'

'Aren't we just going around in circles?' Leo asked. 'Violet has an alibi for Herb's time of death. She was monitoring her kiln. We saw the pots.'

Amelia twisted to look at Barron. He had seemed perturbed when Violet had spoken of the kiln. 'Barron? Do you believe that?'

The big man looked awkward. Violet was his lover, but he knew something. Amelia was sure of it.

'Sebastian Ferver loved Christmas,' he said. Amelia smiled, her heart aching. Her uncle had indeed loved Christmas, but only because he loved giving gifts.

'He liked to buy us gifts. Some of them were small, but some were large,' he continued. 'The last Christmas before he died—maybe he knew it would be his last—he was even more generous than usual.'

'He bought Beatrice a new kiln that Christmas. Is that what you're getting at?' Oliver asked.

'That's how Violet faked her alibi,' Amelia agreed. 'None of us here is a potter. When Violet told us she had to babysit the kiln, most of us believed her, but I noticed Barron looked uncomfortable. Then, when I was in Violet's cabin today, I noticed her kiln was like new. It had all sorts of complicated settings that, I'm guessing, would allow the kiln to be left for hours without the need for monitoring.'

Barron nodded his head vigorously as Amelia spoke. 'I don't know much about kilns; I'm no potter. But I know Beatrice Besson, and I cannot recall a single time she stayed in her cabin to monitor the kiln, not even before Sebastian gave her that new one.'

Amelia smiled.

'Last night, I was at my lowest. As were you, my darling girl,' she said, addressing Daisy. 'But I awoke this morning armed with this fresh clue and half a theory. I thought at length about the cryptic clue in the journals, which at that time I had yet to figure out. And...the second painting.'

'I thought the second painting meant Daisy...' Leo left the thought unfinished.

'Yes, I know what you thought. But you couldn't be further from the truth.'

'Utter nonsense,' Violet said. 'Daisy has already admitted she walked over to David's yacht that night. And then she was out again the following afternoon when Herb was murdered. Those two paintings prove it. How can you be so blind?'

The shadow painter was sitting perched on an upright chair between the two sofas. Amelia approached him and said, 'You painted the first painting of Daisy on Thursday night, correct?'

'I did,' he replied, nodding, eyes boring into the rug at his feet.

'And the second, when did you paint that?'

'Yesterday. Early evening. Certainly, before seven.'

'How? It would still be light at that time,' Amelia asked, though she already knew the answer.

'The back of my cabin is quite shaded by trees, and if I draw back the curtains, I can paint whatever I see through my window.'

'Can you tell my guests what you painted yesterday?'

'A woman in an evening gown, carrying a captain's hat,' he replied.

'But we already know Herb stole Daisy's gown. Although, I'll admit that, for ten seconds after I first saw that painting, I too believed it was Daisy. Then I noticed the light.

'Almost everything in the first painting was darker than the second,' Amelia explained.

'What do you mean *almost*?' Oliver asked.

'When I really studied the two paintings, I realised that everything in the second painting was lighter, except the woman's hair and the dress. It made sense that the tones would be brighter, as it was earlier in the evening. But, if anything, the woman's hair was *darker* than in the night time painting. What could it mean?'

'Well...what?' Maud snapped.

'Don't you see? Two people on this island have a strong resemblance to one another. One with blonde hair and the other a redhead.'

Silence.

'The hair was *darker*,' Amelia explained, exasperated. 'All Leo could see was *another* painting of

Daisy. But to me that was not evidence of her guilt, but of her innocence.'

'Daisy is blonde, and Violet is not. Her hair is auburn,' Maud said, beginning to see the truth.

'Yes. To our shadow artist, who has achromatopsia, everything is black and white or shades in between. He sees the value of light and dark much more clearly than the rest of us...' Amelia sighed loudly, astounded by the uniformly blank faces around her.

'Don't you see?!' she asked, indignantly. 'If it was Daisy in that second painting, the hair would have been *lighter* too.

'Then there is the gown. The second gown was darker than any I had seen Daisy wearing, but it did look like it matched the indigo dress Herb stole from Daisy's room.'

The shadow artist nodded.

'After seeing the paintings, I walked over to the lighthouse and worked out a theory of the crime. We already know that David, out buying a new yacht after defrauding Leo and his chums out of their fortunes in a Ponzi scheme, picked up a copy of *Barco-lona* magazine. After which he hotfooted it over to my little island. Why? Because he recognised someone.'

'Violet?' Wendy asked.

'Yes, he couldn't wait to indulge his sadistic streak by terrorising Violet and perhaps blackmailing her out of any fortune she might still have. David, as we know, liked nothing more than inflicting suffering on others.'

'But what was he blackmailing her over?' Leo asked.

'*Norma will deal with the Hunter $$,*' Amelia answered.

'Explain,' Oliver demanded.

'That was the second puzzle of the journals. Having decoded the reference to *the Hunter,* I asked myself: "who could Norma be?"'

'Norma Jeane?' Price guessed wildly.

'No, and let's not get into a guessing game,' Amelia said with a sigh. 'Lucky for us, as the daughter of Maud Lavender, doyenne of all things stage and screen, I happen to have memorised every word spoken by washed-up movie star, Norma Desmond, in *Sunset Boulevard*. Was Norma Desmond, I wondered, another spiteful reference, this time to an *aging* stage actress?

'It was clear to me that our Norma was taking care of Herb back then by paying him off. But why? And *that* was the moment it all came together. The washed-up actress, Violet, had paid off Herb, aka Hunter S Thompson, to keep him quiet. And now all the players were back, this time on an island too small to keep all their secrets.'

'Keep him quiet about what?' Leo asked, still puzzled by Corey's code.

'Oh, don't you see?' Amelia asked. 'Violet had her toy boy Corey kidnap her own daughter.'

There was a collective gasp. Daisy began sobbing in earnest.

'That's what Daisy realised when she read the journals, though maybe she already knew,' Amelia said, turning to Daisy and saying, '"The actress, the playwright, the journalist, and the Hollywood star went into a bar. What a silly bunch we are…" What did you mean by those words, Daisy?'

'I never wanted to believe it…'

'That your own mother sent a sadistic monster after you, then ran away to this island when there was the faintest whiff in the air that she might have been a part of it?' Amelia finished for her, then turned to Violet.

'You knew Maud was too lost in booze to remember to pick Daisy up from class that day…that is if you even asked her. You also knew Corey was capable of hurting her…you just didn't care.'

She watched Violet's face change, her lips peeling back to reveal her teeth, her careful mask slipping at last. Amelia kept talking.

'You had barely made an appearance in our little drama by the time David was killed, which is why, even when your own daughter's kidnapping turned out to be at the centre of the mystery, even when you gave your little soliloquy about how my Uncle Seb had saved you from the glare of the spotlight after the terrible events that, in your mind, had happened to *you*, none of us thought to suspect you, or even question your alibi.'

'You, Violet, are the one person without an alibi for Herb's murder.' Amelia's eyes bored into the old film actress. Violet gazed emotionlessly back at her. Amelia had always known her to be conceited and arrogant, but this...*this* was unexpected.

Violet's hand slipped into the folds of her dress. Instinctively, Amelia rocked onto her heels, waiting for a reaction. *Any* reaction.

'You bitch!' Violet suddenly hissed, hurling herself halfway across the room, arms outstretched, a knife clasped in her hand. Leo leaped between them, knocked Violet's arm away, saving Amelia from the blade. Violet slammed into him, but before he could catch hold of her, she struck out again—this time at him—before spinning on her heel and launching herself toward the door.

'Argh!' Leo gasped, clutching briefly at his side. Blood seeped through the torn fabric of his shirt, but the wound barely slowed him down as he raced after the deranged ex-Hollywood starlet.

'Don't let her get away!' Amelia shouted, charging behind him.

Always ready to act, Oliver leapt forward with a fire poker in his hand, and as Violet sprinted towards the door, he barred her escape, looking like Fred Astaire in *Top Hat*.

Violet almost crashed into the poker. But Oliver wielded it expertly, forcing her back into Leo's arms, which soon clamped around her waist. With a swift downward thrust, Oliver sent her knife clattering to the ground, and Leo booted it across the floor, a thin streak of blood following it. Wincing, Leo grabbed her wrists as Violet writhed in his arms.

Oliver disappeared into the kitchen, returning a few seconds later holding a ball of cooking twine. He used it to tie her arms.

'Leo, oh God! Are you alright?' Amelia said, afraid to look.

Leo turned and nodded with a wink. 'Tis but a flesh wound, my dear. But it would be grand if someone could fetch me the first aid kit.'

To Amelia's surprise, Tantriana rose soundlessly to her feet and ran straight for Amelia's office. 'Bottom drawer of the desk!' Amelia yelled after her.

'How could you, mama?' Daisy asked, tears rolling down her cheeks. 'Why?'

'Why? Can't you guess?' Violet hissed.

'You're an evil witch, that's why!' Price snapped, pulling Daisy close.

'Evil? Hardly. I was a star! But every new role I was offered became smaller than the last,' she spat, practically foaming from the mouth. 'Soon I knew I would be offered Lady Windemere, or worse, *Miss Marple!* My husband was leaving me...going back to Hollywood. He was done with me. He would continue to pay for his daughter if she chose to stay with me—*if she chose!* But his generosity would no longer extend to my "lavish" lifestyle. Lavish, hah!' She tried to gesture to her current state of affairs, but the twine was tight, digging into her wrists.

'You know as well as I do, dear, a star does not simply just *make do*. If a star is to be adored, she must be *adorned.* I could picture my future...living in squalor, like Maud and her pathetic daughter.'

Maud's arms shot back to her chest as if shot. Amelia nearly flinched at the motion. She was all nerves after seeing Leo's blood.

'My star was waning, and I was losing my meal ticket. I needed to make money fast. Which was when I realised that, while my darling husband might be abandoning me, he did still love his perfect little angel.'

'So, you cooked up the kidnapping scheme with your young lover,' Amelia said. 'Then set up a ransom.'

'The plan was fool-proof and still that idiot, Corey, bodged it. His accomplice, who thankfully knew nothing of my involvement, was arrested. Corey was forced to go on the run,' Violet said. 'And if that wasn't noir enough, that slimeball journalist, Herb, worked it all out. He was going to sell *my* story to the highest bidder if I didn't pay him for his silence. So, that's what I did, even though I knew he would never stop bleeding me dry. Oh, what a horrible greedy man he was!' she hissed.

'It felt like the gods were conspiring against me. I was ruined.'

'But then you were saved, right?'

'Sebastian Ferver, my white knight.' she spat, her lip curled in derision. 'When the rumours started to swirl around me. When Corey's name came up as a suspect, Sebastian offered me refuge here on this god-forsaken rock.'

That was unexpected. And here Amelia thought she'd put it all together.

Why? Why the hell would Uncle Seb do such a thing? How could he!

'He did it for you, Daisy, did you know that? With me out of the picture, he knew your father would smuggle you off to America, far from the slanderous paparazzi who were determined to rake up any muck they could find. Stupid Sebastian, with his soft heart and his ill-founded belief in my innocence,' she said, laughing *at* Amelia, throwing what remaining barbs she could before she was hauled off to Spanish prison.

'He would never have helped me had he known the truth. He was convinced I was as much a victim as Daisy. He promised me it would all die down quickly, and I would be free to return to London, to my life, after just a year or two.

'But then you had to go and get discovered in a shopping mall, of all places,' Violet snarled at her daughter. 'And that first role just had to lead to another, and another...and you stepped into *my* spotlight. And where did that leave me? Now every part of your life was under the microscope; *newsworthy*. If I returned to London, with your fame, that would be too mouth-watering a story for the press to resist.' Daisy cringed at the vitriol.

'Sebastian forbade me to leave. It would ruin Daisy's life, he said, which was when he transformed from my saviour to my jailer,' she complained.

'And then Corey arrived on the island. What happened then?'

'He blackmailed me. Although, knowing him as I did, that came as no surprise,' she said. 'I was at my wit's end!'

'You asked me to sell some paintings,' Barron said, his voice hoarse though he'd barely spoke. *That* was why you needed the money?'

Paintings... It reminded Amelia of the notebook page with a list of his works sitting on his desk.

'Corey was bleeding me dry,' Violet said, not even looking in Barron's direction. 'Then Herb arrived. Of all people, *he* recognised me immediately when I came to the shrine room... You guessed wrong about him recognising David. No, it was *me* he recognised. He followed me, confronted me, and what happened next was a surprise,' she said, her gaze moving from face to face. 'He promised to help me. He told me he was loyal to me—after all I had paid him for his silence. But it turned out to be something else. He had a reputation, an exalted position in Hollywood to protect now.

'Whatever the reason, he agreed to go and talk to Corey, and offer to buy the journals. But when he got to the boat Corey was drunk, belligerent, and instead of helping, like Herb had promised, the fool made things worse by killing him.'

'Was the money in David's fridge, yours?'

'Yes, every penny I had saved for my future—perhaps a return to London and the theatre. That hideous man took it all!'

'So, what happened next?' Oliver asked, sounding bored, which Amelia knew from experience was when he was at his most Pitbull dangerous.

'I had just finished talking to Maud when Herb rushed down the path from the marina, almost knocking me down in his hurry to get away from that yacht. He had Corey's briefcase, but he wouldn't hand it over. Instead, he said he would give me the incriminating papers if I helped him with an alibi. Of course, I agreed.

'We came up with a plan. Herb would get Daisy drunk, take her upstairs and steal something small, some trinket I could take to David's boat to incriminate her. Instead, he took a gown. A gown! And the fool didn't notice she was *awake* while he bumbled around in the dark.

'Anyway, I knew you went down to swim most evenings after dinner, so I went back to the artists' community to find two disguises, including Barron's captain's hat from one of his dress-up chests. That way you would see what we wanted you to see: David arguing with a stranger down on the beach.

'We quarrelled loudly so you would hear and then went our separate ways. Herb took the captain's hat and disposed of it somewhere in the woods, and all that was left was for me to go back and join Barron for the evening and for Herb to find some excuse to go to reception. Voila, he had an alibi, and with the dress I had a handy bit of evidence against Daisy in case I needed it. Maud's nonsense story about wandering into camp just made the whole thing easier,' she sneered.

'Herb agreed to meet me the next afternoon. He was supposed to bring the journals and papers, but he turned up emptyhanded. When I demanded he hand them over, he laughed at me. Called me a washed-out, old has-been. Said he wanted money. I should have known not to trust him!' she said, fists balled.

Her narrative didn't fit the facts. 'There was a bruise from the buckle on the front of Herb's neck,' Amelia said. 'He'd have got that if his killer ambushed him, then strangled him from behind. And you kept hold of that dress... to implicate Daisy in some as yet uncommitted crime—*just in case*. If that's not premeditated, I don't know what is.'

'You can't prove it,' Violet sneered.

'No? If you just went to talk, why were you wearing the dress Herb stole from Daisy?' Amelia asked, knowing the answer.

Violet peeled back her lips, silently snarling. 'You always were such a know-it-all!'

At the sound of her name, Daisy, who had looked more broken with every word, began to shake as tears streamed down her face. Amelia almost wished she had kept quiet, would have done just that if she hadn't sensed that Daisy needed to hear every detail of evidence against her mother if she had any hope of moving on with her life.

Amelia noticed Maud's eyes on Daisy. Then, almost painfully, as if she had aged a lifetime since she entered the room, Amelia's mother placed her cup on the coffee table, walked over to her goddaughter, and sank to the tiled floor in front of Daisy's chair. She gently placed her hands over Daisy's and whispered something too quiet to hear. Daisy made a keening sound Amelia had never heard before, and hoped never to hear again, as she doubled over to rest her damp cheek on Maud's hands.

Amelia felt the sting of tears in her own eyes as she cleared her throat, her gaze never moving from the two women. Maud must have heard the sound because she shifted her attention from Daisy to Amelia. Amelia didn't know what her mother saw in her face. Perhaps she saw a changed woman, one bolstered by the satisfaction of solving the crime and—fingers crossed—saving her inheritance; or maybe she just saw the same old Amelia.

But she did know what she saw in Maud's as she listened to the noises of Violet being escorted out of the room. For the first time she could remember, Amelia saw compassion for someone other than herself mirrored in her mother's eyes.

CHAPTER FIFTEEN

Amelia sat at her dressing table. In front of her, leaned up against the mirror, was the painting of her father she'd found in the shadow artist's room. Beside it were the three passports she found on David's boat, and beside those was the key on the gold chain the monster had been wearing around his neck.

Jordi, Estell, and Mar had arrived a few hours earlier, and when they did, they'd immediately radioed the police and Violet had been carted off to a prison cell on Mallorca. After that, it had been all hands on deck to prepare food and drink for the gala.

Which brought Amelia to now, sitting at her dressing table that had once been Sebastian Ferver's writing desk, as she put pearl studs in her ears and finished applying her lipstick.

There was a knock at the door and Daisy poked her head around it.

'Can I interrupt?' she asked, still half hidden by the door.

'Of course. How are you feeling?' Amelia asked, stretching her hand toward her friend.

'I'm better than I thought I would be. Like a weight has been lifted,' she replied, crossing the room to stand beside Amelia's chair.

The two women's eyes met in the mirror. They both smiled.

'Isn't that—?' Daisy said, pointing to the painting.

'Yes, it's my father,' Amelia replied, not wanting to talk about it. But Daisy's attention had moved on. Her eyes were glued to the little mound of curled chain and the key resting on top of it.

'May I?' she asked, picking up the chain so the key dangled from it.

Amelia hesitated. Daisy seemed calm now, but it was just hours since the poor woman had been sobbing in Maud's arms.

'There's an...engraving,' Amelia said, her voice hesitant.

'What is it?' Daisy asked, grabbing the key and squinting at it.

'It's your name.'

Daisy's winced, going pale, but she kept hold of the key.

Amelia didn't know what to say, but she knew this was a make-or-break moment for Daisy. 'He kept you prisoner with that key,' Amelia said. 'He still held you captive, even after all these years. But now you hold the key to your own destiny. You are free of him, and you can be free of his legacy too, if you want it.'

'That's what I came to tell you. I'll stay for as long as you need me to—just to be sure you meet the terms of the Will—but after that I'm leaving. Peppy is taking me somewhere. Somewhere secret where I can do the work I need to, so I can kick the drugs, so I really am free of him.'

'Oh darling, I'm so happy for you. If I can—'

'Lia, you've done enough for me. This last bit I have to do on my own. But I'll be back here to see you, better and stronger. You'll see,' she said as she turned away from the mirror, the chain still dangling from her fingers, and crossed to the door.

'I need to get ready now. I'll see you downstairs,' Daisy said as she quietly closed the door behind her.

Amelia turned back to the mirror, fastening the second pearl into the lobe of her ear, her mind still on Daisy and her struggles with addiction. She was facing the battle of her lifetime if she really wanted to kick the pills that had staved off her fear of the darkness all these years.

The monster, David, had been addicted too. *Yes, she thought, addicted to the thrill, and to his own image reflected in the tear-filled eyes of his victims.*

And then there was the poor, aging Hollywood starlet, Violet, so addicted to fame and adulation that she had conspired to have her own child kidnapped.

And what about Leo, who had shared the pain of loneliness he had felt with the death of Sebastian Ferver. What was his weakness? *He's hooked on believing.* Leo would ignore the evidence of his own eyes and ears in order to believe in the truth and goodness of others. He believed in Dominic Strathclere so deeply that his good name had been ruined, and he had believed so deeply in Maud's lies that he hadn't even thought to ask Amelia for the truth. Yes, Leo's belief in goodness had caused as much damage as any addiction.

As for her, Amelia knew her need for certainty was a crutch. But she thought, with relief, she had lived through the most uncertain year imaginable; her uncle's death, her inheritance, two murders... Yes, she had lived through uncertainty and survived it.

Half an hour later, Amelia was dressed up to the nines, waiting on the front step outside the grand entrance hall as her party guests began arriving from the marina. They were delivered by a grim-faced but suitably resplendent Oliver in his Land Cruiser.

Although she knew he would be arriving to verify she'd met the terms of her uncle's Will, she was surprised that Alfred Boustred, the solicitor, was one of the first to clamber out of the back of the Land Cruiser.

He was sombre, incongruous in his black single-breasted suit as he processed, solemn and sedate, across the driveway, pausing briefly to shake her hand and murmur his congratulations before continuing to the hotel. Amelia remained where she was, greeting each of her guests personally, and directing them into the grand foyer where they would be met by her newly returned staff, offered a drink, and escorted into the drawing room where the party spilled out onto the terrace.

Her hand was stinging from all the shaking when the last of the stragglers eventually wandered inside. Amelia didn't follow; just watched as Oliver parked his Land Cruiser discretely on the far side of the circular driveway, then ambled back to stand silently at her side. Together they breathed in the evening air.

'They're both in the drawing room?' Oliver asked.

'Yes,' she said, her gaze never moving from the sparkling lights of Mallorca in the far distance. 'In accordance with darling Sebastian's instructions, we have built a hotel, gathered together a menagerie of guests for a grand opening, and my two childhood friends are now ensconced in the drawing room, chatting amiably with the Chief of Police over a glass of very expensive champagne.'

'So, you have bested his challenge. The island is yours.'

Amelia nodded. 'And for you, a million pounds... What will you do now?'

'A million doesn't go far these days,' Oliver faux-mourned, his lips twitching. 'I don't think I'll be giving up my day job, for now.' Amelia released a breath, raised herself up onto her tiptoes, and planted a kiss on the tip of his nose.

'Shall we?' he asked, putting out his arm for her to take as they turned and walked inside.

For hours Amelia played her hostess role to perfection, mingling, chatting, topping-up a drink here and an hors d'oeuvre there, and while she did it, Albert Boustred lamely chased her in circuits around the terrace.

'What are you doing?' Maud asked, appearing out of nowhere at her side. Amelia, whose nerves had had enough of a pounding for one day, jumped six inches into the air.

'Just savouring this moment of peace. Albert has been practically chasing me around the terrace, trying to get my attention. No doubt he wants to formalise my inheritance. But the funny thing is, even after working so hard for it, when he speaks those final words, it feels like Sebastian Ferver really will be gone.'

Maud nodded, then asked, 'She's gone?' Amelia frowned. 'Daisy,' Maud clarified.

'Gone and not a moment too soon...for any of us.'

"*Lia,*' Maud hissed.

'I know, I should be grateful and ladylike and exuberant. But I'm not. I'm exhausted and sad.' She was more than sad; she was bereft.

'Yes, poor Daisy,' Maud replied, misunderstanding.

'Price is taking her directly to a treatment centre without passing go' Amelia said. 'It is apparently the first time she has managed to amass enough strength to attempt it. No doubt, she'll be back in Hollywood in a month or two, where she'll force herself to forget this new trauma, and in the process, she will forget we exist...again.'

'Perhaps, or she might surprise you,' Maud said, waving at someone behind Amelia.

'As you have, Mama,' Amelia said. 'I did not expect you to charm sweet Wendy into giving you another go.'

'I was quite surprised myself,' Maud agreed.

Amelia didn't know which of the two women had met their match. She was just grateful her life was here now, and not in London.

In the years after Maynard's disappearance, Amelia hadn't known how to break away from her mother's scotch-soaked misery without hurting the woman as badly as it hurt Amelia to watch her slow decline into an abyss of her own making.

Leo thought Amelia had stayed because she had been brainwashed into self-hatred and masochism. It was true she had listened to half a lifetime's worth of Maud Lavender's particular perspective on politicians (elitist scoundrels and gaslighting monsters), religion (wrong-headed charlatans), classic literature (overrated in the extreme), and the weather (practically unliveable, whatever guise it came in), that most of all she had listened to her views of her daughter—a clueless, often clumsy, plain-faced fantasist.

But Amelia had never believed Maud's lies. She had always known that Maud needed to focus on the defects she saw in others to distract herself from her own much more obvious shortcomings.

She knew they were lies because, for the first eight years of her life, Amelia had been blessed with Maynard Ferver as a father. A father who had gloried in his daughter's beauty, her intelligence, her lust for life, and her sparkling personality. And the day after he disappeared, her Uncle Seb had turned up at their London townhouse—a youthful Oliver at his side—to continue Amelia's education.

After the events of this week, Amelia sensed a change in Maud—perhaps not a big one—but a change nonetheless. Which had her thinking of another change in Maud, fifteen years earlier, on the day she had supposedly forgotten to collect Daisy.

'Are you sure Violet asked you to collect her?' Amelia asked, cautiously.

'Daisy?'

'Yes.' Amelia nodded. 'I had no idea you were meant to collect her that day. Not until Daisy let it slip yesterday.'

'It wasn't exactly something to brag about, was it?'

'No, it really isn't. But it just seems strange that I didn't know. I was responsible for your appointment diary and fielded all your calls,' she said. 'There was no call that I know of, and no reminder in your diary.'

'She made it up?' Maud asked, aghast. Taking a step backwards, her face was a mask of horror.

'I think she must have. To deflect attention,' Amelia said, then watched her mother's eyes fill with tears as she absorbed the knowledge like a blow. Her mouth opening and closing noiselessly, Maud turned and dashed off into the melee.

Eventually, like the inevitability of the changing seasons, the old lawyer discovered Amelia's hiding place.

'Amelia, at last,' Albert said as he approached. 'Is there somewhere we can we talk privately?'

Amelia nodded, taking hold of his arm and steering him inside. Once in her office, he settled himself on one of the comfortable visitor's chairs, while she shut the door then took her seat behind the desk.

'Amelia,' he began, 'I cannot express how delighted I am to see that you were able to meet the terms of your uncle's Last Will and Testament.'

'Thank you. It has been something of an adventure, particularly the last few days. But we managed,' she replied.

'Quite so. All of which means it now falls upon me to read a second document, a letter, provided to me by Sebastian Ferdinand Dunnicliffe Ferver to be read in the event you were successful in your task.' He rummaged around in his document case for a few moments, frowning and muttering, 'Where the devil is that letter?' before withdrawing an envelope with a *ta-da* motion, holding it outstretched between them. He took hold of her letter opener and sliced it open.

Amelia realised she was holding her breath. This would be the final communication from her uncle, a thought that brought tears to her eyes.

'Do you know what's in it?' she asked. Alfred shook his head, unfolding the pages.

'Shall I?' he asked. Amelia nodded, unconsciously taking hold of the edge of the desk, as a climber might grab hold of a rock to prevent themselves from falling.

'Yes...' she replied through dry lips.

My darling girl,

I knew you could do it! Alfred said I should write you a separate letter in case you failed. I told him, "Poppycock!" That's how confident I was in your brilliance and ingenuity.'

Amelia smiled. *Poppycock.* How typical of Sebastian Ferver to curse like a Victorian gentleman.

'I have so much to tell you, but I can't think of a good place to start. That's why I started with congratulations.

'I suppose the next thing I should do is explain the nonsense in my Will. It was hastily drafted, and I know you must have been hurt by my stipulations. But there was method in my madness, darling.' It sounded strange to hear her uncle's warm endearments spoken in Albert's dusty tone.

"*A year ago, something happened to convince me to leave my paradise, return to London, and put my affairs in order.'* Amelia rather thought, as Oliver had once intimated, that it was her suffering that had brought Sebastian home. But perhaps not...

"*And by putting my affairs in order, I mean that I must find a way to expose at least some of the secrets I have gathered over a lifetime. I fear there is no time to tell everything. My strength is fading.*

'There are other secrets that are so damning—so dangerous—*that if they were released or fell into the wrong hands, they would be ruinous to everyone involved. It is these secrets that are the real legacy that I entrust in you, and they are hidden here on my island.'*

'But back to the Will. I am sure you will know by now that Beatrice Besson is, in fact, Violet Forrester. Originally, I brought Violet here not for her own benefit, for I strongly suspect she had some part to play in poor Daisy's ordeal, but to protect you and Daisy from her

toxic influence. I often wish I could have spirited Maud away to the same purpose.

'But, of course, that could not be. With Violet, I can't deny I was torn between searching out the proof so that she might be punished for her crimes, or protecting Daisy. It couldn't be both. You will have your own thoughts on my actions. May God forgive me if I have been wrong.

Amelia was ready to explode. Though, why she was surprised by Sebastian telling this story in the same rambling, shaggy-dog way he had done when she was a child, she did not know.

'What I know of Violet's story, and the stories of many others, are contained in my files which I have secreted away...can you guess where?' Oh yes, Amelia knew where to look for Sebastian's secrets. She was sure she would find them in the same place she had found every one of her Christmas presents when she was a child.

The caves.

'But now I must turn to sadder matters. Did it surprise you to learn that, knowing I was dying and returning to London, I did not contact you? I'm sure it did. But you see, about six months ago, my health, which had been quite marvellous, began to deteriorate quickly and inexplicably. I have tried to pinpoint when it started—it was the day after Christmas, a day when Jordi the cook, Pau, Oliver, the six island artists, and I had been playing games and sharing gifts. I felt quite peculiar and took to my bed. After that, I'd have good

days and bad days, but the trajectory was ever downward.

'It took a long time—too long, it turns out—for me to realise I had been poisoned.'

Albert gasped and stopped reading. He stared at her, aghast as she snatched the letter away from him, scanned the page for where he left off, and continued reading.

'Poisons. Some work instantly, so that whoever is there with you must be the murderer. Others build slowly, nibbling away at your essence like a mouse nibbling at a mountain of cheese.

'This island is small. There is no-one here who I have not broken bread or shared a cup of tea with. No-one but Violet. For, whilst I cannot be certain of her involvement with Daisy's kidnapping, you can be sure she made her anger at me obvious enough to have avoided her presence, let alone any food or drink she might have offered me.

'What you may not know—although knowing you as I do, I suspect you will by now have some inkling—is that all the residents on the island are here because hiding the evidence of their secrets would have been insufficient. These people have secrets so dark that I must contain their very persons here.

'Don't blame Oliver for any of this. He knows some but not all of what I have done, and he has chided me regularly for acting like God by interfering in people's lives.

'Which brings me full circle for the cloak and dagger terms of my Will. Knowing she was not the poisoner,

I determined to set events in motion that would force Violet's crimes into the light, while at the same time, bringing you two girls back together at last.

'Although I had no concerns as to your immediate safety, being quite convinced that Violet was not my murderer, I decided to be cautious and send you Leo. You had once been so close, and I was determined to give you some support through the inevitable stress of the challenge I had set for you.

'But there was some possibility of danger. Someone had gone so far as to murder me, after all. Jordi, Pau, Oliver, and the six artists.'

Six? There were several extra cabins over in the community but there had only been three artists this past year. Oliver would know who the others were.

'As I write, I am waiting, here in my sick bed, for the results of test that will prove what I am saying. My doctor, Bill Palmer, has been given permission to share those results with you...and only you.

'And so it is that I bid you farewell, my darling girl. I am sorry to place this burden on your shoulders. Remember you can always trust Leo.'

The letter ended abruptly. That was it—the last communication she would ever receive from her dear uncle.

'Ahem...' Albert muttered, stretching at his collar. 'That was...*remarkable.*'

It was past midnight when Amelia staggered out of the office. She stumbled, shell-shocked, up the staircase, and rushed across the landing and into her suite.

Once inside, she walked to her dressing table, sat down, and pulled open the drawer. Inside, amongst the normal detritus, was a writing pad.

She scrabbled around in the drawer for a few more moments, searching for a pen, and when she found one, she began writing a list. A list of names of people who might have murdered her uncle. Her heart was pounding, and her eyes stung at the thought of it. Someone had murdered Uncle Seb, and he had written her a letter, calmly explaining how he thought it might have come about.

Amelia swept away an angry tear with the back of her hand as she wrote: *Oliver, Barron, Hank the shadow artist, Jordi, Pau, Estell, Mar.* She was chewing the top of her pen thinking when Leo strode in without bothering to knock.

'Is everything alright?' he asked. 'You've been gone a long time. People are leaving, Oliver is showing others to their rooms. And still the band plays on.'

Amelia noticed Leo looked healthy enough. Oliver had patched him up, his first aid skills reaching well beyond those needed for grazed knees. Though to Amelia, he still looked a bit peaky.

'Oh dammit. I had a lovely speech planned, thanking you all. But I got waylaid by Albert and then...' She didn't know how to break the news to him.

She sat quietly, reaching for the right words, when Leo interrupted her thoughts. 'We need to talk about the painting, Lia.'

'I know,' she said. 'But not now. I've just had some...disturbing news.'

'From the lawyer?' Leo asked, looking worried.

'He was murdered,' she explained.

'They both were,' he agreed. 'Though I'm not sure I can summon a great deal of sympathy for either of them.'

'No, no. I'm not explaining myself properly. I'll start again,' she said. 'Albert has just read me a letter from my uncle. I knew there would be one. Uncle Sebastian loved me, and after that horror of a Will, he had some explaining to do. It's just that...' Her hand shook as she reached up to tuck her hair behind her ear.

'It's what?' Leo asked, reaching out to take her hand.

'Uncle Seb said the people on this island had secrets, that he'd brought them here for their safety, or maybe the safety of others... Anyway, he said there was evidence hidden down in the caves and...'

'And what?' Leo asked.

'He said... Leo, Sebastian thought *he* had been murdered. By someone on this island. Poisoned.'

Leo's face froze in horror. *Oh dammit, I didn't get it right at all,* she berated herself.

'Poisoned?' Leo croaked.

'Poisoned,' she confirmed. 'And I've been sitting here, wracking my brains as to who would want to murder the most precious, protective, loyal, and loving man I have ever met. I don't even know where to start in answering that.'

Leo stared at her in silence, his face tight, his eyes bright, as if he was absorbing a blow as painful as that delivered by Violet just hours earlier. When he spoke, his words were a salve to Amelia's frayed nerves. 'If Sebastian thought he had been poisoned...I believe him.'

Amelia nodded. She believed her uncle too.

'And if we are both agreed on that, it is up to us to find out who,' he continued. 'So, Amelia Ferver, super-sleuth-extraordinaire, somehow you managed to uncover the crazy goings on of the past few days. What makes this new mystery any different?'

'It happened over a year ago,' Amelia grumbled. *And* three of the artists who were living here are now gone. Moreover, I have no idea who visited the island over those last months of Uncle Seb's life. It's all so complicated, Leo.'

He stood quietly, waiting for her to recover her equilibrium; waiting to remind her of something she already knew but had apparently forgotten.

'He'd do it for you,' he said quietly. 'He wouldn't make excuses or question himself. Sebastian Ferver would not leave this injustice unpunished, and that being the case, nor can we.'

He's right. Sebastian would be on their trail already, she thought. 'But what can we do?'

'If you were writing a play, what would the sleuth do now?'

Amelia took a second to consider. 'First, we search the caves,' she said. 'Then, we head to London to talk to Uncle Seb's doctor.'

THE END

If you are intrigued to find out how Amelia solved the mystery surrounding the death of Malcolm the stagehand, you can discover the truth in this newsletter exclusive novella, A Killer Observation. Click on the image or go to https://www.ameliafervermysteries.com/a-killer-observation to get your free copy!

Acknowledgements

First and foremost, I want to thank my patient-beyond-reason husband, who shouldered far more than his fair share of household chores while I figured out how to write a mystery novel.

Next, there's Dustin Bilyk of the Author's Hand, who mentored me through that learning process and edited the final manuscript.

Last, and very far from least, are my first readers: Lynn and Phil from my writers' group in Menorca; my lovely beta readers, Cary and Lee; and Stuart, my downtrodden husband, who always provides the last set of eyes before the novel goes to print.

I thank you all for your kindness, professionalism and loving support.

You Rock!

Printed in Great Britain
by Amazon

THE CURSE OF THE HIGH IQ

By

Aaron Clarey